T0193654

SAND

A HISTORICAL NOVEL

RAYMOND WINSON & ROBERT FEATHERER

authorHOUSE®

AuthorHouse™
1663 Liberty Drive
Bloomington, IN 47403
www.authorhouse.com
Phone: 1 (800) 839-8640

Published by AuthorHouse 09/18/2018

ISBN: 978-1-5462-6073-8 (sc)
ISBN: 978-1-5462-6072-1 (e)

Library of Congress Control Number: 2018911206

Print information available on the last page.

Any people depicted in stock imagery provided by Getty Images are models,
and such images are being used for illustrative purposes only.
Certain stock imagery © Getty Images.

This book is printed on acid-free paper.

To my beloved wife Jenny, your encouragement and faith in me is beyond any measure of description. To my "daughter Jen", how blessed I am to have had your help and candid input.

To Dave Chase and Lisa Booth you both have meant so much in this effort, God bless you. To Bob Featherer my partner and friend of over half a century, wow! Hold fast shipmate, the voyage has begun!

To my wonderful wife of 51 years and growing who pushed me forward in my Naval and civilian careers to make me succeed and to my kids but in particular to Rick who always showed an interest in my Navy life. To Ray, an unequalled friendship.

Characters

Lieutenant Frank Christmas — Pilot/SMA199513

Jenny Soliban — Fiancé to Frank

Sam Colby — Director of FEMA/SMA19651

Kitty Colby — Sam's wife

John Cunningham — Deputy Director FEMA/SMA19652

Steven Story — U.S. President

Logan Arnold — President Story's Chief of Staff

Marty Windham — Personal secretary to President Story

Alex J. Cord (AJ)	U.S. Vice President
Jane Graham Story	First Lady
Paul K. Webster	U.S. Senator
Blair Jordan	Aid to Senator Webster
Mark Salerno	P3 Co-Pilot
Admiral John Carter	Commander-in-Chief Pacific
Hai Jun Shang Xiao (Captain)	PLAN Commander Hainan
Hai Jun Zhong Xiao Dong (Commander)	Executive Officer Hainan
Hai Jun Shao Xiao Chung Hui Li (Lieutenant Commander)	Senior Watch Officer Hainan
Hai Jun Shang Wei (Lieutenant) Chun	J-8 Pilot
Li Jaing Hua	PRC Ambassador to USA

Premise:

A band of fraternity brothers, deeply committed to keeping the United States of America as the reigning world superpower, become alarmed when they learn that the President of the United States permits the passing of highly sensitive (and heretofore classified) military missile technology to the government and military of the Chinese Communists. The brothers view this as an open act of treason and covertly plot to neutralize the exchange and cripple the People's Republic of China's Command and Control Communications (C3) system with a sophisticated computer virus.

However, If unsuccessful, it could produce unintended cataclysmic consequences on an unsuspecting world.

Fraternity, n: (1) a body of people associated for a common purpose or interest; (2) a group of people joined by similar backgrounds, occupations, interests, or tastes; (3) a chiefly social organization of men students at a college or university; (4) a solidarity; (5) the quality or condition of being brothers; brotherliness.

Chapter One

He was sleeping when the call came - a stirring ring of reality almost lost in his unconscious dream world. Although awakened instantly from his deep sleep, he didn't stir, he didn't move, his breathing never altered. His training kicked in; even in the doldrums between sleep and consciousness. If anyone was in the room, it would appear that he remained completely oblivious to the phone ringing as well as to their presence. He slowly cracked an eye open to observe his surroundings; his ears pricked for foreign sounds. The room was dark; nothing was out of place or unusual. He was alone.

The telephone rang a second time. He slowly reached out and silently lifted the receiver and placed the phone to his ear. He did not speak. A monotone voice, void of gender identification, said, "Time".

Without replying, he replaced the receiver back on its cradle, rose silently, clicked the bedside lamp on and visually inventoried the entire room again. He mentally clicked off the room's contents as he had before retiring the evening before; everything was normal as it had been for months. Everything was in its rightful place.

He moved silently to the bathroom and removed his bed clothing. He turned on the water and showered, first icy cold to shake the cobwebs of sleep and then scalding hot to completely resurrect himself for the day's work ahead of him. He shaved using an old-fashioned straight razor, and uncommon fixture in today's world yet one that could be used for a variety of other functions without raising undo alarm with its possession. As he toweled himself dry, he observed his scarred body, only lingering in certain areas where he recognized the scared remembrances and reminders of his profession.

After dressing inconspicuously, yet purposely, in dark slacks, light blue shirt, and plain tie, he rechecked his preparations which he had practiced on a daily basis. His belongings were sparse as he was prepared to depart the apartment on a moment's notice knowing that, when the action day occurred, he would never return. Like every other morning, he meticulously began removing all evidence of his presence; trash bags were filled with personal items, clothing was bagged unceremoniously. Using rubber gloves, he wiped all possibilities of his finger prints from every surface, paying particular attention to the windows, the telephone, and any other item he may have handled. He followed every protocol for survival; he removed his presence from the room, from the apartment, from the building, as if he was never there.

Today was the day, the real thing after months of waiting. The phone call had finally come, **the activating word for which he had so desperately anticipated**. The repetition of his daily routine had occurred hundreds of times; but he calmly waited for this, his one word tasking.

With briefcase in hand, he exited the room, glancing over his shoulder one last time. Nothing could remain; he must vanish without a trace. He had lived there for **what seemed like an eternity but only spanned seven months in real time** and had taken great pains to establish himself as insignificant, a non-entity, a mousy little businessman coming and going without fanfare. Every day he arose and followed the same nondescript procedures. He could be the manager at local soda fountain or a salesman at an aged bookstore. Equally, with his adherence to his "uniform" style of dress, he could be a Wall Street senior executive. His daily departure established a routine that any witness would dismiss as ordinary. Even the landlord knew little of his existence and lifestyle but remained thankful that the rent was paid on time and, most significantly, in cash. That cash payment allowed someone else to take advantage of the system and skim what they could off the top before reporting to the Internal Revenue Service. What a country – everybody took their little piece of the pie, either legally or illegally and most importantly, got away with it.

He wondered if he was the only one or, would there be others of whom he was unaware. His years of training emphasized compartmentalization of information – the less he knew the less he could compromise in the event of capture and ultimate mission failure. His mind wandered back to the three maps that he had memorized in anticipation of the call. That one word "Time" initiated his mission, designated his destination and sent how many more assets he did not know about, in motion.

Outwardly, his departure on this autumn day was like that of any day in the past seven months. The weather was predicted to be chilly yet bearable; the forecast would cause people to dress in layers so they could remove their heavier outer garments as the day heated up. Cheaply and inconspicuously dressed with briefcase in hand, he differed little from those around him and truly hid the intent of his business. But, today his true mission started – once completed, would forever raise doubt about this democratic government and change the political direction of the United States for generations to come. He did not, however, know now but his actions, on this day, would be debated for decades.

His briefcase was not that of a businessman, instead of folders, notes, and paperwork, the case was altered and especially designed to conceal the true intent of his business. His case was much heavier to carry than a normal briefcase so he had practiced carrying it and exercised for months to ensure that the average observer could not distinguish the difference between it and the average business man's prop. Inside the nondescript case was his weapon of choice, a specially designed .223 caliber rifle. A very special rifle not purchased in any sporting goods store or specialty gun shop. There was but one purpose for this rifle, it was the rifle of an assassin. He cleaned it daily in anticipation of its use. Broken down into five sections - two of the sections were seven inches in length, one section was fourteen inches long with the silencer and scope a mere six inches long each. These five sections, along with 12 rounds of ammunition, were designed to fit in the case in a manner that allowed for quick assembly and an equally fast breakdown. The ammunition was specially designed, the mercury tipped filled bullets would ensure death striking anywhere near a vital organ…He had mastered his rifle and was able to hit a quarter sized target at nearly 600 yards in a 15 mile per hour crosswind and in very low light. He was ready. His photographic memory allowed him to memorize all the data relevant to his mission. His destination was close, yet far enough away from his pseudo home to separate him from the apartment. No connection; no traceable information to aid in any identification.

As he neared his destination, he paused briefly to clear his mind. Concentrate! His moment was now and he could not let his benefactors down. He knew the brotherhood was strong – they would take care of his family as promised – a family that had slowly began dying off years ago. His mother was all that remained and her age had reduced her to a shell of the person she once was. After the sudden death of his father, she had aged even more quickly. She had had to give up her home – the place where the family had grown up. His father did not leave her much and she now dwelled in a home for the aged and infirmed; a place that demanded more financially than he could handle. But, the brotherhood stepped in and provided more than enough to cover her bills in payment for his dedication. With a successful mission, he too would benefit financially and be set for life in Singapore posing as a research analyst for the Academy supposedly studying the warlords of the Far East. An apt ruse, studying warlords who had left their mark on history would find him taking an anonymous albeit a major place in history.

Snap! Bring it home, get back to reality! His arrival time was critical; not too early to allow his presence to be conspicuous; not too late as to miss his target which was scheduled between 12:15 and 12:30 PM. His shot would be slightly less than seventy-five yards **moving** from his left to the targets right. One shot, one kill; how strange life was. From his position on the grassy hill, history would be changed In an instant and would be forever clouded with suppositions and, speculation, indeed this would be a November neither he nor the nation and even the world, would ever forget.

With an impact such as this, he thought his nerves would get the best of him. Yet, he was remarkably calm. He knew he would be successful and he had no thoughts of regret. The plan was well conceived and all he had to do was to aim the rifle, put the President of the United States in his cross-hairs, and squeeze the trigger. It had to be done. The President was preparing to make a deal with the Soviet Union; a compromise the President thought would benefit the country. Yes, but whose country? Not ours! The brotherhood was right, you don't make a deal with the devil, so Kennedy had to be stopped.

Today was November 22, 1963. SMA195413 was going to see it through. Failure was not an option. God Bless America.

Chapter Two

Sand Military Academy was located in Morristown, North Carolina and provided the Tar Heel State's equivalent to the prestigious Virginia Military Institute of its neighboring state to the north. The sprawling campus was situated at the base of the Cape Fear River that served as the gateway and principle transportation route to the interior of North Carolina during colonial times. Its namesake, Cape Fear, served as the southernmost point of the state and, as a result of shifting currents, formed the Frying Pan Shoals, part of the ship graveyard of the Atlantic.

Within reasonable travel distance, the Marine Corps Base, Camp Lejeune, near Jacksonville, provided a direct link to the active military and served as a backdrop for many of the military training activities undertaken by the Academy. As home to the II Marine Expeditionary Force, 2nd Marine Division, the Marines provided the "Hoorah" example so necessary to "fire-up" the students of Sand. What better outfit to represent the history of the United States military than the 2nd Marine Division which was originally formed before the outbreak of World War I. Their history was resplendent, the perfect example for students to follow; from WWI through WWII; Belleau Wood,

Chateau-Thierry through Guadalcanal, Tarawa, Saipan and Okinawa. As every American knew, there was no better example of discipline and military demeanor than that presented by the United States Marine Corps; just the sight of a Marine in his dress blue uniform instills patriotism and order, traits that served as the backbone for the Marines and Sand Military Academy students.

Sand Military Academy made every attempt to establish uniqueness with its presence and its culture but, at the same time, it required relationships with established elements in the United States. The Academy was modeled architecturally in the Jeffersonian style, yet retained the gracious southern ambiance so prevalent to the surrounding community. There were, however, no Confederate flags; **there were little or no statues depicting the heroes of the South.** - Sand sought to solidify allegiance to the Union. Sand graduates were not limited to, but included some of the most prominent civil servants and military leaders in the history of our great Union. The curriculum was diverse yet strict in military, mathematical, and technical disciplines. Sand's professors all sustained one driving force in their efforts to produce the best men and women to the United States - their goal was to instill ultra-patriotism throughout the student body; and unquestionable patriotism to ensure that the Union would never be subjected to the threat of a future Civil War like that which destroyed approximately 620,000 human beings, more than all other wars in which the United States was involved in from the Revolutionary War through Vietnam.

Similar to other military academies and colleges throughout the United States, Sand academic alternatives ranged from liberal arts studies through biochemistry and nuclear physics. Commensurate with this wide range of academic choices were the social clubs and fraternities, who through their applied academic theory and zeal for superb resolutions to the nation's problems strove to manifest a better world. Unique to Sand Military Academy was the "Epsilon Phi Upsilon" (E Pluribus Unum - Out of Many One), fraternity, a very secretive brotherhood sworn to preserve and defend the United States against all enemies both foreign and domestic. Specifically they pledged their combined efforts in perpetuity against all insurrectionists and treasonous persons without regard to the targeted entities title, status or position or to the personal cost required of any Sand member selected to eliminate the problem.

At its inception in 1906, Epsilon Phi Upsilon numbered 13 original members. Its stringent eligibility requirements mandated that a brother could only remain in the fraternity as long as they kept their pledge; the slightest deviation would result in an automatic expulsion. This stringent requirement was revalidated as often as necessary to ensure its compliance. In keeping its secrecy intact, brothers were identified by their class year and a sequential one-up number coupled with the initials of their name. With these identification characteristics, a frat brother could remain in touch with his fraternity sibling regardless of the time passing since graduation from the Academy. Beginning with Sand Military Academy's inception, this fraternity wove a slender thread through history that would connect time and events as only a master tailor could weave.

Thirteen men (representing the original thirteen colonies) served as its officers; a President, Vice President, Judge, Upper House (four members), a Lower House (four members), a chaplain, and a Sergeant-at-Arms. These thirteen, at the end of their term, would personally sponsor their successors and were identified by a special alphanumeric code to distinguish them from other fraternity members. Each officer is identified as SMA (Sand Military Academy), year of graduation (all four digits), and a personal sequential number relating to the position held, i.e. President would always be number 1; the Vice President always number 2. Continuing with this scheme, judges are designated by the number 3 with members of the Upper House designated by the letter "U" and the Lower House by "L" preceding their numbers. Lastly, the Chaplain and the Sergeant-at- Arms would be designated "12" and "13" respectively. Thus, the class of 1906 Chaplain would be designated SMA190612; the same officer in 1942 would be SMA194212. When referring to one another, abbreviated forms such as S4212 (Sand, year of 42, position 12 or Chaplain) would be used as identification.

Under no circumstances would names or titles be tendered to ensure the anonymity of the officer. At the completion of their tenure, each officer vowed to never join any organization, social or otherwise, that could provide insight to their connection to Epsilon Phi Upsilon. Rather, their anonymity would always be protected by their ability to remain as fringe people, rarely seen and seldom heard. This further provided their insulation from any covert action that may be sanctioned. No one would ever know, for instance, that S5413, was the mysterious "grassy knoll" entity that ended the life of President Kennedy, a fact which never surfaced despite years of investigation. Equally, no one would ever know how S651, S652, and S9513 kept the United States from the brink of unrestricted nuclear war.

Chapter Three

The Oval Office, as part of a complex of offices located in the West Wing of the White House, has changed with each president's personal tastes and requirements. Although in theory, the White House belonged to the people of the United States, it assumed the personality of the incumbent and changed with the election of each new President. Since its inception in the early 1900's, furniture, draperies, and even the design of the Oval Office carpet changed with the election and subsequent arrival of the new President. Paintings adorning the white walls of the President's primary place of work are selected from the White House's collection or borrowed from museums for the current President's term of office. The three windows facing south and the four doors leading to different parts of the West Wing remain a constant and provide the President and his staff easy access to other parts of the White House.

Today, the Oval Room was resplendent in representing the American people - the gold drapes covering the three windows; the dark blue rug with the presidential seal emblazoned in the center of the room; the Stars and Stripes stood proudly to the left; the Presidential flag to the right. Roses fresh from the White House garden's private stock were displayed on both credenzas; their aromatic scent wafting throughout the room. The current President was a plant freak so hearty greens were everywhere. He always preached that lots of plants meant the production of good air - something to do with science and natural air cleansing **(at least he thought so)**.

Today was a normal day. Half empty coffee cups and a half empty box of Dunkin Donuts (while the White House staff normally provided confectionary items, the President always preferred Dunkin Donuts; his favorite being the coconut covered donuts) cluttered the coffee table in the middle of the room. Working papers, some emblazoned with dark red ink indicating their security classification, were strewn all over the top of the President's antique Resolute-style desk as well as the coffee table. Some had even managed to silently slip to the normally spotless rug. No one cared – it was a working day and work it was.

President Steven Story, like his predecessors, listened to his advisors and staff on a far ranging list of topics. From simple things such as the invitation list for planned state dinners to more complicated issues such as the reaction of foreign powers to U.S. actions and increased seismic activity in the western region of the U.S. **At times, these people seemed more worried about dinner knife and fork placements than the increasing size of the fissures in the earth threatening the people of southern California!**

His staff was replete with super egos and every one of them had what they thought to be the definitive answer to all of the issues piled high on the presidential plate. Their opinions were supported by information collected, cataloged, and dissected by the largest intelligence network in the history of mankind before they were presented to POTUS (President of the United States). The National Security Agency's (NSA) budget had deep pockets. Since its establishment in 1952 by then President Truman, NSA spent its money wisely (**although** sometimes without oversight) to effectively produce information quickly, quietly, and accurately to ensure the President had all the information for his decision making processes; those involving both foreign and domestic issues. **It sometimes seemed almost hysterical to watch and listen to their discussions cascade in to near screaming matches right in front of the most powerful man on earth! Eyeballs resembled those following a tennis match, back and forth until someone called fault and then all eyes turned to him, the umpire!** It **did**, however, **remain** his responsibility to digest the myriad of data presented to him, formulate a decision and ensure it was carried out for the benefit of the country and its citizens.

Yes, the presidential job had more perks than one could ever imagine but Harry Truman's "the buck stops here" quote placed the responsibility right where it belonged. Once opinions became decisions, right or wrong, he, and he alone was responsible because, no one would care about the underling's opinions. **As he looked around the room, the President often wondered why he, or anyone else would want this job. The pay was lousy - you could not even sit on the toilet without someone accusing you of doing something wrong! Most of the House hated you, the Senate was always looking for a way to file impeachment charges and, me, I had to put up with a whining wife to boot! Oh well, such is life.**

On this day, **the news media had** President Story **in the headlines** for the wrong reasons and **his own stupidity elevated him to the front page and the opening story on the evening news. While he would not openly admit it,** this too was his responsibility. **His tenure as President had produced a history of half-truths, sexual innuendos and front page pictures on all the magazines and newspapers in the supermarkets and drugstores. His approach this time would be the same as always, it worked before and would work again.**

Play everyone from the media to the consumer! News, what is news? In the United States, news becomes relevant only when it sells a sponsors product or provides a 'gotcha' for the reporting agency. Truth? Does it matter if truth somehow gets presented or whether variances of the truth, or for that matter, complete falsehoods, are emphasized from those "reliable sources" which are somehow never identified? Truth was abandoned when celebrity opinion became more important to society than fact, innuendo more important than concrete eyewitness corroboration. When the opinion of a Hollywood actor concerning world events holds more weight than that of those dedicated to national objectives, we can establish that both the society and the country are crumbling into ruin, and sadly may even be beyond restoration. Equally, one must ask why the sexual escapades of a morally misguided young woman in this country demand front page headlines and a never ending following of paparazzi to document their meaningless dribble. The truth? The truth is, sex sells! It sold in the past, is selling in the present and, undoubtedly, will sell in the future. It has, after all, provided a host of insignificant, unimportant people with their fifteen minutes of fame, vaulting the heretofore nobodies to the front page, however fleeting. Its titillating indiscretions have many times brought the high and mighty to a ruinous end.

President Story was currently involved in just such an "indiscretion".

His latest dalliance would not lie down (no pun intended); it just would not go away. If sex sells, this story currently resided atop the bestseller list. In some parts of the world, his actions would be considered normal for a man of his power and position. The woman meant absolutely nothing to him; a mere diversion from the daily grind of high power of Washington politics; but here the fifteen minutes of her fame would be multiplied a thousand fold. The indiscretion with a young and infatuated secretary was nothing new to presidential politics, and denying it was all that the ideologues wanted, but swearing he didn't even know the girl and then having the security logs provide her signature as visitor to the Oval Office on numerous occasions, well... sex plus President equals never ending headlines, the more deviant the better, the more detailed, the greater the story.

A wry smile crept on the face of the President as he thought of his real job for the day - discredit the press. Turn the tide and get the people to believe in him and with the help of his trained hit squad render impotent those who attempted to smear him and his legacy. The fact of the matter was that although there were some powerful, party-friendly people out there, the press lived for the scoop, the front page; video at six and eleven. The demise of the right or left administration was equally acceptable. In his eyes, the press had tried to malign both he and his administration since his first term as President. If the press was so pro-liberal, how did the news of his rendezvous with the leggy young secretary get out? Who was it blundered the story in error or planted the seed depicting the President as nothing more than a sexual deviate who placed his own satisfaction high above that of his family and administration. From the side of every politician inside the Washington Beltway, the ultimate name of the game in D.C. was defeat (or perhaps softer, malign) the press. He was better at it than most, and took great pride in his ability to turn scandal into harmless boyish slips that everyone seemed to enjoy and laugh over as well as forgive.

Bob Pate, the President's Press Secretary, felt the best way to defuse this specific situation was to ignore it, the girl could be bought off either with a few thousand dollars or threats on her personal well-being or both. Pate's staff would swear to anything Pate told them to say and do; the almighty press had nothing if they weren't spoon fed everything...why give them any kind of basis to provide more information to the pathetic public? Ignore it; today's headlines would line the bottom of birdcages tomorrow and bird crap would obscure the print and be tossed without fanfare. The official White House statement would be "No comment", just like the descriptions of all his discretions of the past.

The President of the United States hasn't got time to waste on unsubstantiated innuendo and suggestions of presidential improprieties. The White House needed a crisis of a different nature to sway the headlines to a different level. Where were those idiots in the Middle East when you needed them - on any given day, somewhere in the Middle East, various factions were blowing something up and killing and maiming many of their own people as possible. Attack this, attack that! Their purpose had little to do with life; their only attempt was to dress the front pages of newspapers worldwide in the efforts to sway political and personal satisfactions. Muslim versus Muslim, Arab versus Arab, who in the West really cared! It really only mattered if the price of oil went up or down as rising oil prices got more attention than the death of 100 people in Iraq! Too bad the efforts of the myriad of terrorist organizations or one of at least a dozen other wacko groups wanting to kill everyone over there did not surface this morning.- where were they when you needed them? If they would just blow a few more things up or kill a few more people, this whole sex issue would go away - second page news today and then the fade into oblivion. Maybe the earthquake thing could be turned into a meaningful diversion. The President didn't have time for these exploits - He was focused on the seismic instability out west demanding to be kept up-dated hourly if need be of any change no matter how insignificant. **After all, those tall buildings out west were beginning to sway, pictures were falling off the walls and dishes were popping out of cabinets; people were beginning to get concerned.** This would help keep him insulated from the press searching for scandal.

If it wasn't the Middle East crazies, what about the war-mongering government in North Korea? They had played saber-rattling political games with the United States since the end of the Korean war in the early 1950's For every U.S. and South Korean venture, the North Koreans had a trumped up political counter-attack. NSA expressed worry over the North Korean's military and intelligence capabilities for years. After all, with the Chinese Communists help, they waged war against the United States for nearly three years and, due to U.S. fears of another world war and subsequent non-action, had held their own. For years, the North Koreans had waged cyber war against the U.S. and their intelligence system tested our capabilities daily. As a matter of historical fact, the U.S. and North Korea and signed a truce so they we still technically at war with our country. **Above all, the North Koreans still had one of our ships, the USS Pueblo ((AGER-2) tied up in their harbor and were using it as a tourist attraction!** The same North Koreans seemed to have the Chinese Communists in their hip pocket and would milk that possession for everything it was worth.

With all that said, today, the most important thing to President Story was the focus of the press elsewhere.

President Story wanted out of this political storm; he wanted out of Washington for good. After one and a half terms in office, the President, no, the man (a huge difference), was tired of pretending and putting on this "I really care" act when in reality, he did not!

Each of his surviving predecessors lived lives of the rich and/or famous, supported by the American people for the rest of their lives – most were already rich and additional monies would become available with writing their memoirs and experiences while in office. Every ex-President erected "his" library which came close to breaking their own arm patting themselves on the back for such a great Presidency while they were in office. President Story, however, wanted more than that. Notoriety was not his concern; he would rather live in anonymity as long as he was filthy rich to allow for his fantasies to become realities. Money indeed was the root of all evil but it must have been a rich man that could buy anything who coined the phrase. From his initial entry into the political arena nearly sixty years ago, President Story established himself as a political powerhouse using whatever means necessary, legally or illegally, to undermine his adversaries and promote himself. Promises here, promises there, were made and broken to serve his purpose of self-promotion. His back-stabbing and elimination tactics were fully recognized and feared in the back alleys of high powered politics.

He did not limit himself to those of his own government right, or left, but had established his ruthlessness world-wide; those who dared oppose him were broken using tactics established throughout time; blackmail, sex, drugs - you name it, if it provided input to his personal coffers, it would be done. He had amassed a huge sum by anyone's standards but he would need at least three times that to live his remaining years doing the things he wanted to do, perhaps most importantly maintaining his power, bowing to no one. He could easily skim eighteen to twenty million in "donation" money away, it wasn't even a challenge. His tactics forced his adversaries to support him. Those who challenged were quickly reduced to non-entities. To meet his wild dreams, he would need to score big. Neutralizing the effects of the Central Intelligence Agency and the Federal Bureau of Investigation had gone a long way to ensuring that his actions could never be traced back to him. The Chinese had been making persistent overtures and served as a strong possibility for a future score; the catch was what they wanted in return for a mega donation. He had to act soon or all could be lost. While in power, Story could persuade the Senate and the House to grant China favored nation status. Doing so would open unlimited Chinese imports and conversely, open China's doors to American technology. Their interest in military applications and associated technologies would be the route to his success. Everyone would come out a winner and loosen the famed Chinese purse strings. In turn, he could manipulate these additions to his own coffers - open the front door while working an end-around to ensure covering his rear and further neutralizing any U.S. watchdog agencies.

He needed to make contact in a wide-open way and still ensure that his suggestion would bring the desired results. Perhaps a state dinner would provide the platform he needed to soften the Chinese stone faces. Their penchant for saving face would be the very door that would let him extract a very large donation from their piggy bank (he laughed - did the Chinese even have a piggy bank?), he'd get what he wanted all the while letting them think that they would be running the show - make them feel important while slipping money from under their noses. He'd have to do this one himself - he would ask for one billion that would leave plenty of negotiating room before he hit his rock bottom price. He would hang around for two or three years and then, at the end of his term, "retire" to a country without extradition rights sans Mrs. Story. He could after all not take the proverbial ham sandwich to a banquet; and international playground, somewhere in a warm climate - sun, sand, sex and unlimited wealth. Yes a heaven on earth, no press, no work – just beautiful young island women on some tropical island serving him and his maladjusted colleague's alcoholic beverages for his remaining days.

He laughed out loud. He needed to get through this latest discretion and those that would obviously happen down the road. He laughed again. Story had a penchant for real gold, good whisky and the golden company of the fairer sex.

Bob Pate would be his savior once again. Without question, he always was.

Chapter Four

Ambassador Tao Hua saw his chance and boldly laid his proposition out. If the United States would approve the transfer of some technological information, the benefits to each would be obvious. He would have to use all his abilities and every asset to ensure his desired progression.

His hidden agenda; his reward - he would be advanced to the inner circle of the Party Leadership. More importantly, he would be solely responsible for co-opting a sitting United States President on the Chinese payroll, and directly placing him under his thumb. Through his plan, coupled with rapidly advancing Chinese technology now almost on par with the decadent West, he would go down in history as the world figure who had knocked the United States off of their self-created pedestal and reduced them from a super power to that of a second rate nation, second behind his beloved China. His country's technological advances had raced them to the forefront of the scientific world. These advances must be transferred to military capabilities and provide specific countermeasures against the military machine of the United States, a gap which had to be narrowed to ensure future successes. Chinese intelligence services were dedicated to breaking the barrier of U.S. security and acquiring the classified information concerning U.S. missile and anti-submarine warfare advantages currently held by the West. Eliminating these advantages were the highest priority in China.

His plan, would, initially, make him appear as perhaps the biggest political and "face" loser in all of China's history. Yet, slowly he would evolve as the Master Planner and lead China to the brink of world domination. In the beginning, the President of the United States would benefit from every conceivable financial situation imaginable; he would benefit behind the scenes, and amass a fortune well in excess of his greedy intentions. He unknowingly would then be lulled to sleep; like always, President Story's success would be introduced to special treatments. His lust for young lotus flower maidens would provide the stage for the slow but systematic entry into drug induced states of sexual bliss, that once begun, would ensure a deepening reliance upon the drugs and submit him to the complete control of Tao's realm. Once the puppet was on the string, Tao's commands would ensure that the United States was nothing more than a lackey for the Chinese government. His inevitable downward spiral to the ever more potent Chinese drugs would alleviate any further financial obligations, and would in fact bring the lost pay-offs back to Chinese hands and then his financial inability to sustain the addiction would keep him on the tether. He must hurry however, President Story's administration had only two years left in power.

Once this transition was accomplished, the Chinese government could then deal with the traitorous rebels on Taiwan and Chinese hegemony of the entire Asian area would be completed. China's position in the world would be as it was meant to be, destiny had always intended and the Hua family would forever have power like no one had ever dreamed of - the Chinese would tell stories and sing songs of the Huas. What good luck to have been born at this time in history, to become the most famous Hua of all time! The trick would be to place himself and the President of the United States in a position where only the two of them could talk - in a private setting with no one else around. Only then could the offer be made and only then would the trap be set, only then!

Ah, perhaps the Bilderbergers could then be of use. With their control of the press and other media sources, to say nothing of western politicians and business men, they could manage private introduction to the American President on less formal terms. His past well-hidden and well-placed investments were long past due for a payout. This would be the perfect time to demand payment. Tao's hands were sweating and he was breathing hard. This was what intrigue and international diplomacy were all about. He pitied those who were mere amateurs at this or that - they would never enjoy his successes; never. He summoned his aide to the room.

"Get my western clothing ready", he nearly shouted. "We must schedule a trip to Canada immediately. Tell my wife I will be gone a minimum of two weeks, then let my cousin, Choy, know that I will need the services of his special friend with little or no notice".

Tao's aide scrambled to the walk-in-closet. His clothing was arranged neatly by fashion attributed to different parts of the world. He began selecting the western style clothing carefully, ensuring to cover both formal and informal wear. Ambassador Hua continued, almost ranting.

"He is to be ready to fly to Canada on my call and to have his access to hard U.S. currency for transfer to the Swiss bank account at my direction".

"Do you understand"?

His aide nodded, afraid to make a sound. Tao's wrath was easily initiated and out of complete fear, he complied without hesitation.

"Go"! "Prepare my trip and make NO mistakes"!

How providence has smiled on him; his mother would be so proud if she could only know the intricacies of his plan. She had taught him well; he was an eager student. For many, many years however he did not think it would happen; he did not even fully understand but, now the prize was easily within reach. A bigger gift than he had ever dreamed. The execution of his plan would be flawless and his confidence was high. After all, he prepared for this his whole life; the golden moment was near.

He had so many times heard the phrase "God Bless America" from the Western cronies who thought of him as just another "s!ope". Well, he had a counter saying, "God Bless American stupidity". With this coup, the words fit the situation in much grander style.

Chapter Five

The Federal Emergency Management Agency office of Director, Sam Cosby (SMA19651) often left its visitors in awe. It was like visiting a display at the Smithsonian Institute; a shrine to the family of a dedicated government worker. Every available space on Sam's desk, walls and bookshelves were vested with pictures of Sam, his wife Kitty and their son, Frank. However, the office was totally void of the usual plaques and citations earned by such an accomplished veteran as Sam. No pictures of Sam and the President or the presentation of awards or medals by reigning dignitaries; nothing like that. Sam realized that most callers to his office considered him to be just a bit obsessed with his family, just a L-I-T-T-L-E over the edge.

Sitting at his large mahogany desk, he had lost track of his current chain of thought. He knew too well that family unity, loyalty and trust in today's world was all too much a fleeting condition. As he smiled at the latest picture of Kitty, Frank and him, his thoughts drifted to a time years ago.

He thought about Frank and how he and Kitty had felt on the adoption taking place on Christmas Day when they could combine the celebration of the Christian holiday and the anniversary of Frank's adoption together for the rest of their time on earth. The papers had been signed, sealed, and delivered and little Frank would soon come under their charge. Their only remaining decision necessary was that of a surname. Frank hated his given name of Arora and he wasn't overjoyed with Cosby. As an eleven year old, he wanted to establish himself as unique and not to necessarily take on the name of his adoptive parents. After many long and thoughtful discussions it was decided that the only name that made any sense would be the last name of Christmas, Franklin Thornton Christmas.

Over the years, Frank was nurtured by the Cosby's and he grew and became the son the Cosby's never had. Bright, articulate and very goal oriented. Nothing could deter Frank from his goals. Once he had set out to accomplish a task, it would be done. **After Frank completed his Naval Academy graduation, he immediately applied for flight school where he completed all his aerodynamics, aviation physiology, engine and navigation testing in Pensacola, Florida. Following primary flight training, he was assigned to the P-3C Orion four-engine maritime patrol aircraft squadron and trained at the Naval Air Station in Corpus Christi, Texas. Franks was then selected to fly** the Navy's P-3 Orion anti-submarine warfare aircraft as Lieutenant Frank Christmas.

The knock at the door startled Sam and brought him back to reality. While he did not know exactly where Frank was, he knew of his deployment to Japan and that Frank would fly in close proximity to both North Korea and China. He often times would imagine that Frank would have an air mishap and wind up missing or presumed dead, lost at sea, or, even worse, shot down over North Korea or the Chinese Republic and was a prisoner. **He remembered stories of an EC-121 reconnaissance aircraft being shot down over the Sea of Japan by a North Korean MIG-21 where 31 Americans were killed in the late 1960's.** But, such was the life of being in the military of the United States; **while everyday seemed dangerous to those performing their duties, everyday had a mission and everyday was dangerous.** While normal citizens respected our military they had little knowledge of the everyday hazards facing those who voluntarily wore our military's uniforms.

John Cunningham (SMA 19652) entered the room without being acknowledged and, before Sam could collect his thoughts, was standing right in front of the desk,

"The news is not good and is far worse than we expected", John nearly shouted as the door slipped shut.

Sam's heart moved in to his throat. No, he thought, not Frank!

John continued, "POTUS had just approved the outright sale of highly sensitive missile technology to the Chinese. This move would give the Chinese full parity in missile defense and full knowledge of the offensive capabilities of U.S. systems."

Sam remained in that gray area of time; somewhere between what he was thinking, what was being said, and what he was hearing.

"Sam?"

"Sam! Did you hear what I just said?" asked John.

"Thank God!" Sam uttered. All that was on his mind was Frank.

"What do you mean Thank God. I just told you the President is giving the Chinese Communists everything they need to hamstring us and that is all you can say?" a frustrated John continued. "What is your problem?" "We have to do something and do it quick."

Initially, John Cunningham, along with many of his contemporaries, thought it all a hoax or even better just Washington rumor. Our President, with all his think tank advisors **could not and would not** be dumb enough to compromise the most advanced offensive and defensive missile system in the world.

Before coming into Sam's office, John had vetted the information through his contacts in the Department of Defense and State. The information **was double-checked and confirmed** and, unbelievably, would soon be released to the press and the American people. Within 24 hours, the Chinese would possess our secrets, our capabilities, and our countermeasures. Was the President an idiot? Had our government lost its ability to reason? Worse, **was** our President a traitor?

Without the President's knowledge, that goofy little intern he was involved with was **a counter-intelligence agent and was providing** counter-intelligence officers with information **with which** they had been able to confirm that the missile system data transfer was being conducted **both** openly and clandestinely with the approval of President Story. **The President's intelligence and counter-intelligence community was not as naïve as all expected after all.**

"Sam", John yelled, "what are we going to do"?

This is a city where no one gave anyone time to think. People in key positions were supposed to have answers mid-way through the sentences coming out of the mouth

of those asking the questions! If you could not handle that, you did not belong in Washington, D.C.!

Sam pushed his chair away from the desk and walked over to the window where he looked out over the city from his 5th floor office window. Do? Do? His mind was racing as he quickly contemplated what the result of such a transfer actually did mean... If the Chinese had parity with U.S. missile technology in three years, then all bets would be off. They would not hesitate to establish a strangle hold on Taiwan and for that matter anything else they wanted in the Far East, the Spratlies. Indeed, this was a gravely serious incident that was equal to the Kennedy thing back in '63, but taking out a sitting president today was a far cry from what it was back then. That would not be a solution to the problem this time. But, they had to have something that would absolutely slam the door shut on the Chinese, still giving the President more than credible deniability and even more; ensure that this would never happen again.

"We have to meet with all the particular parties as soon as possible", Sam responded. "There is little or no time to spare. This has to be squelched as soon as possible."

This was definitely going to be an effort that could not include CIA, State or any of the other normal players. It had to present itself as totally believable, give the Chinese something that they couldn't resist and yet destroy every bit of technology they would soon be using against us. How in heavens name do you do it in a matter of months?

An executive meeting of the committee must be conducted with as little fanfare as possible. It would take a day and a half to get the necessary people together. Under the guise of a trip to the Outer Banks, which was close to the

Academy as well as Washington, DC, would provide cover for the meeting. The one and a half days would also provide the opportunity to lay out the problem and devise a solution that would, for once and for all, to stop this traitorous trend of the Story administration to destroy mankind's best hope for nuclear restraint.

Sam picked up the phone and called his wife. Kitty came on the line at once. She was used to these last minute calls of "I won't be home for a couple of days; something has come up and needs to be dealt with right away. I'll make it up to you when I get back; promise". He hated doing it but it had to be.\

As he gathered his papers, Sam said to John, "John, get hold of the others, all of them, and let's get going" "Set up our cover story and demand full attendance – no excuses. As soon as the story breaks in the press, everyone will further understand its importance.

Thirty minutes later, after several telephone calls, Sam and John left the office.

Chapter Six

Kitty Cosby hung up the phone. No surprise. After years of Sam's government service, she knew and understood these spur of the moment dashes to meetings in unknown places were indicative of serious problems. While Sam never talked about his work, she knew that these meetings would be followed shortly thereafter by headlines on every newspaper in the country indicating some type of government crisis. Don't think the wives of government workers were not knowledgeable of what was going on; they weren't stupid – two and two still made four.

Life goes on, daily chores continued. She had wanted to clean out the back bedroom closet even since she opened the door a few weeks ago and things fell out all over the floor. The Cosby depository held things that had been hidden for years. She poured herself a glass of iced green tea and started he chore. When she opened the door of the closet, a small box of old photographs tumbled out onto the bedroom floor, spilling the contents helter-skelter, in all directions.

Kitty knelt down and started picking them up, one at a time, giving herself the luxury of strolling down memory lane for a moment or two with each photograph, she looked at each slowly realizing what a truly blessed life she and Sam enjoyed.

Their first home, at Snow Hill Apartments, in Laurel, Maryland served as their "home base" while Sam served a tour of duty at the National Security Agency, sometimes called the Puzzle Palace or Disneyland East. Fort Meade was a strange place back then; no gates, no military guards. **The strangest "military base" in the entire country**, in fact, you could drive on the Fort via Route 198 or Route 32 and be on and off the base before you even knew it. **It seemed like you could transit from a civilian town, to an Army Post, and back to the civilian town without a wisp of military police or military presence but, don't try exceeding the speed limit because the Military Police would nail you in a heartbeat! The most formidable building on the entire base (or Post as the Army called it) was that of the National Security Agency which was not hidden from view but plainly announced on traffic signs coming off the Baltimore-Washington Parkway. Seemed extremely odd for an agency which wanted to mask its identity rather than advertise it.**

She vividly remembered the day of May 15, 1972 when Alabama Governor, George Wallace was shot four times **by Arthur Bremer on that sunny Monday afternoon at an outdoor rally in Laurel, Maryland.** She even remembered watching the ambulance taking Mr. Wallace to Holy Cross Hospital in Silver Springs. He survived but he would never walk again. **These type of things stay in your mind forever.**

The photograph she was holding mostly reminded of her life style back then and how some decisions that long ago would affect their future. It was tough to survive financially back then. She remembered eating lots of hot dogs and tuna fish – their surf and turf – on their small budget. It was there that she and Sam first started talking about adopting a child. They discussed the differences between adopting a baby (for which the wait would be longer) or an older child which would be available almost instantly. They agreed on how special an older child would be as so few older children could get out of the system and in to an actual family.

Funny, she hadn't thought a minute about the memories of the closet, just the accumulation of junk. Her tea gone she refilled her glass and sat down on the bed to begin to take a more serious nostalgic journey, and with Sam gone for who knew how long, she could afford the luxury of the trip. She would start with dividing the photos into groups where they had been assigned, then she would try to remember which photo took place before the next - a good test for her memory and a very practical way to arrange the photos.

Just after they had adopted Frank, they instituted what was to become significant daily event, "family time," not that they had worked out some magic formula that would help them bond, but she and Sam did feel that Frank must have lots of things held back and this would at least be an attempt to bring them out without a third degree interrogation of the boy. Each night for one half hour, they devoted time to each other. Each night a topic was chosen for discussion, they ranged from her favorite recipes to Sam's passion for sports, and each gave their total devotion to the little sessions. Not many weeks into the routine, the discussion of religion came up. The questions young Frank posed were not easily answered like, how did God come into being and why did

He allow evil to exist? What happens when you die? Is there really a heaven and a hell? Would he know his biological parents in heaven? **All of these questions were not easily answerable for the two of them and they required the outside help of some religious counselors.**

She hadn't been keeping track of time when the phone rang she cleared her mind and checked her watch. Midnight, where had the time gone? It was Sam.

"Hey, Kat, I'm probably going to be gone a couple of weeks, sorry I didn't get a chance to talk very much, I must be getting too old for this stuff anymore. I didn't have an opportunity till just now. I'll be down in Nags Head and I need you to pray for us. We're **really** up against it this time."

She couldn't figure out whether it was due to fatigue or what, but Sam had never asked her to pray in quite that way before. His whole tone sounded strained and unusual.

"Of course I will, Sam", she instantly uttered a quick offering up to God… "Please God, please give Sam the wisdom and courage he will need for whatever it is he needs it for."

"I love you, Kat."

"*Love you* too Sam".

They hung up and she looked down at the floor and decided she needed to stop where she was, tomorrow was another day, and she'd finish then. **Too many memories were filling her mind and she did not want to be without Sam.**

Chapter Seven

First Lady Jane Story fumed. Once again her glandular, adolescent husband had brought folly to his presidency. She had dedicated herself to occupying the White House ever since her sophomore year at college. She didn't marry for love, she didn't date for love - love had nothing to do with real life, she knew if she positioned herself rightly an opportunity would come.

At first there would be small things, committee seats, maybe as a mayor someplace, a run for a state office then maybe Governor or a Senate seat if things would just work right for a little while. A few well sponsored agendas would give her the national recognition she deserved and then she would have a legitimate shot at the Presidency, a "first", a woman contender for the White House.

Jane mentally drifted back to her first time in the White House as a child tourist, seeing things that thousands before her had seen on the guided tours of the "American people's house". Even as a young girl, she was awed by the elegance of the place and, even at that age, vowed that time would provide her the opportunity to control its operation. Jane Story would have her own impact which the future would provide. Her influence would pale that of even Jackie

Kennedy who re-established the ambiance of the place during her three plus years as the First Lady before her husband Jack had been struck down by an assassin's bullet.

Jane's initial impact as the First Lady **began immediately**. Her **effect** would be ten-fold in the future **when she became** President! In that capacity, she would control everything **from the color of the curtains in every window to the identity of every aide in the White House** because there would be no "First Man" of the White House during <u>her</u> tenure as President. There would be no man in her private life at all; **she did not need one**. The only men in her life would be those surrounding her with professed loyalty to her as POTUS. All she had to do is keep herself in the spotlight until the idiot she was married to finally had one little escapade too many and the people would remove him from the presidency, the party would cast him off as a liability and that would clear the decks for the betrayed loyal and dedicated wife to strike out on her own. The fool, he was as conniving a man as she had ever met, the problem was that he was more inclined to use his wiles on some unsuspecting young waif than in the political arena where he could have so easily dominated for as long as he liked. Well, let this be a lesson to all women, men were useless. He probably wouldn't even apologize, just go on denying and denying that there was any substance to the accusations.

She knew he was lucky that the press adored him. They'd by-in-large **given** him a pass, but not her, oh no, not anymore. She didn't marry him to be his personal damage control officer for the rest of her life. **Her** personal agenda outweighed anything her "husband" could imagine. She had accepted the indignities, the cruelty of a loveless and embarrassing marriage as well as his sexual forays with any women who would consent **to the President of the United States** at a moment's notice. **These "ladies" had a personal agenda also, they would be able to brag to their families years in the future with a seemingly medal of "look what I did with the President" hypothetically pinned to their chest.** He honestly believed his charm was the mitigating factor in all his affairs but it actually little to do with his amorous abilities. Little did he know that having an affair with a man of his power and in his position was the catalyst for the egos of the women who dared to go beyond all acceptable standards of propriety.

It would seem that only an international incident of the grandest scale could defuse this one. The Middle East or Far East might be good for something after all. She realized how wise she had been to hold off with any retaliation against him, he would have to follow her lead again to extract him from this trip down teeny-bopper lane. She mused that to nullify a crisis, one first had to find a crisis.

She called for "her "Personal Security Advisor", Chuck Halstrom.

"Chuck, I want everything hot on the Middle and Far East immediately. Bring that press guy over here, too. We're going to try and inject a little international crisis to deflect a national calamity".

She grinned, soon enough the White House would be hers and she could dump "Jimmy Bob" She would rule the roost and he could go to his little hen house and stay there for all she cared. **The wheels continued to turn.** She had decided to drop his name and resume her maiden name. It even sounded more presidential.

President Jane Grayham!

When she divorced him she'd probably pick up a million votes for that alone. **Women would sympathize immediately and even some of the men would swing her way for the way she was treated by her uncaring spouse.** It always amazed her how in the United States men were always depicted as being the better leaders and managers, **yet,** what did men know? **This was not the 1950's when woman were always placed in second rate positions and depicted as incapable of making well-thought out decisions. Men, however, were** so busy trying to get intimate with every woman that they met. She had accidentally married a political gold mine; it was hers and she naturally wanted to capitalize on her good fortune. C A P I T A L I Z E,

President Grayham.

President Grayham, she rolled the words over and over again in her mind,

President Grayham, President Grayham, oh how she loved the sound!

President Grayham. She'd lose her husband to infidelity which would offend some and as always, there was still many purists out there who would cast their votes accordingly – poor Jane, but in the end because she had suffered so long she would emerge triumphantly the winner of the next election, oh yes, make no mistake, Jane Grayham was not going to be denied.

Madam President! No matter how you said it, the word President before her name sounded magnificent.

The doorbell rang.

Chapter Eight

Senator Paul Webster thumbed haphazardly through the small mountain of paperwork on his desk. Although he performed the routine daily, the pile never dwindled; contrarily, it always seemed to grow. He discovered early on in his career that sifting through his 'personal" mountain of government paper work would unfailingly uncover another issue to keep his name in prime time – a position critical to his goal of making a run at the presidency. To ensure his quest, he would need to be careful not to lean too far to the right or left; he needed to balance his position between Republicans and Democrats – fair enough to please each side but to equally ensure he did not overstep his boundaries and upset the balance. Balance was the key; uncover corruption (of which there was plenty), attack it give it no quarter, trophy hunt - winner take all! He had been totally successful so far by using this formula; keep your allies friendly and your enemies off balance while at the same time keeping that even keel. The art of selective whistle blowing to feather one's own cap should be offered as a college course in political science. The objective in the United States' educational process would be to ensure newly emerging politicians could get a hefty pay off in the long run.

Page after page, he scanned the paperwork until he reached a somewhat obscure looking financial review document. FEMA spending had risen nearly 28% in the last 18 months. **Interesting. w**hy? His near perfect memory did not alert him to any specific reasons or of any natural disasters or man-made circumstances which would cause such a rise in spending. He felt he was just about to insert the key into another scandal and unlock the wrath of his relentless persecution of any party involved in such an activity as…the knock on the door broke his chain of thought yet he knew intuitively that he was on to something.

"Excuse me Senator, his page sticking his head in the door your immediate presence has been requested on the Senate floor, I don't know what is going on but I know it's a doosie."

"Thank you, young man. Please inform the ranking senator that I will be there post haste".

He returned quickly to the report as the figures continued to bother him, what problems existed that would cause such a severe increase in spending? His instincts, honed through years of experience, indicated something was seriously wrong **but he had to get to the Senate floor immediately**. He closed the report and placed it carefully in his briefcase. He'd look in to this in much greater detail in the near future. Twenty-eight percent increase! FEMA was a bureaucratically run office that responded directly to the President and responded to natural disasters and recovery. Their government bankroll controlled billions. He jotted down a few notes on the cover of the report.

FEMA – Director?
Deputy?
Budget?
Expenditures – last 5 years?
Staffers? Ambitions?

His thoughts continued as he closed and locked his office door. How often had some obscure report resulted in heads rolling at all levels of the government. People in our profession always seemed to think that as long as it was reported, regardless of vehicle, it was OK and no one would notice. It was an excuse to cover ineptness or error, legal or illegal. With the potential of exploitation and bettering his position, he would have to use extreme caution; to reveal any wrong doing too early would leave him open for misinterpretation and attack. To reveal too late, could be interpreted as a possible cover-up.

He would assign Blair Jordan, his best and most ruthless aide to vet the report with specific instructions for confidentiality. It could be an interesting week indeed. Oh how he loved Washington, DC.

Chapter Nine

Ernesto Sharp was a happy man. The son of a Cuban mother and American father, he had used his God-given analytical abilities to attain a Bachelor's Degree in computer science and supplement the under graduate degree with a Master's Degree in computer security. Not far down the line was his Doctorate **(Dr Sharp did sound pretty impressive)** which would assure him of a promotion at the highest level of computer development and security within the U.S. government **and** its support from government contractors. Achieving that success, he would be capable of ensuring his parent's future and allow them to enjoy the financial successes they never experienced as young adults.

Ernesto felt just as accomplished with his successful contributions to SQUALL (the navy's latest venture into computer directed anti-submarine warfare attack). His analytical capabilities and conversion of technicalities into common sense and easily understandable language had proven to be an asset throughout his career. This was a major boost to his current company – the acquisition techniques alone were worth a fortune. As always, the United States had technical capabilities far in advance of the rest of the world. The Soviets, the Chinese, the North Koreans and every other potential enemy of the United States would spend millions on espionage to acquire even minor information on such capabilities. Even the Arab community would be interested, not so much for their own benefit but for the ability to acquire such data and sell it on the open market to the highest bidder.

SQUALL worked. It could track submarines anywhere within the footprint of its satellite imagery. The United States had invested liberally in the satellite systems which now circled the earth and supporting the system to the point where it had coverage of nearly 90 percent of the globe. After years of research, its capabilities were expanded to the detection and tracking of missile launches not only from undersea craft but from hardened launchers as well. Most significantly was SQUALL's ability to pinpoint the exact location of a target, albeit missile, submarine or surface platform to within yards of its location at any time during its voyage or flight.

Acoustically, it was so sensitive that it could detect minute differences in the natural biologics of the ocean and the anomalies associated when a man-made object was inserted in to the "detection zone". This zone and its search area were then analyzed for biologic content using a sifting program which categorized the zone and matched it with all possible biologics that could naturally enter it. Anything that did not match was identified as a "hit" and assigned a preliminary number. Super speed diagnostics then evaluated the hit and, if it did not correspond with an accepted profile, a second nano-scrub would be performed and a master number would be assigned. Once the master number was assigned, target tracking would engage which, in turn, automatically activates weapons release engagement. This whole process took place in mere seconds of the hit.

SQUALL was impossible to defend against, once locked on to a target there was nothing that could stop it. No amount of avoidance or countermeasures could prevent the final outcome, the total destruction of the intended target. With an effective operating range of over 500nm, SQUALL was the shield that U.S. Naval forces needed to **continue as** the world's dominant sea power,

To Ernesto's surprise **(and to that of the entire program all its research)** was that simultaneously, and quite by accident, SQUALL researchers produced the perfect computer virus; a virus so insidious that once it was opened, every time a computer systems anti-virus scan was engaged, the bug would debilitate the ant-virus scan so that it would eventually be rendered useless. Within six to eight months of operation, the system would not notice the introduction of de-generators and at approximately 1 year, the system would be rendered totally defenseless and permit hacking to reverse every operational program. Any attempt to regenerate new systems from existing programs would be impossible leaving the attacked system operators no choice but to replace everything. Knowing this information, a potential attacker would know exactly when computer controllers command defense systems would be open for exploitation. The attacker would then enter the system and extract all operational supplanting an override which would, at the click of a key, shut down everything.

While the classification of SQUALL and its capabilities was of the highest level within the United States security system, the classification of the accidental virus discovery was even higher; one which officials contemplated creating a separate and distinct security protection level. The capabilities of the virus were compartmentalized and were afforded further limited distribution even within the compartmentalization. The ability to introduce such an undetectable virus into an enemy's cyber world with the capability to destroy a country's entire computer system **had** to be protected.

Introducing the virus would be the difficult part of any mission. Of course, this information would not be kept secret long – but sometimes even the threat of a virus would have computer operators everywhere edgy. Now, how to, would be the goal – the, when, was as soon as possible – the, why, because that's how we stay on top – life was good – and about to become momentarily unequaled.

Ernesto was proud; he had every right to be. His efforts, along with a few others, had produced the most lethal weapon known to man short of a full-out nuclear blast. In essence, the U,S, now had the ability to completely render enemy submarine forces impotent. The system could be launched from air, surface or subsurface platforms, thereby allowing the U.S. to establish foreign policy with the mere hint of what could happen with non-compliance.

Chapter Ten

Lieutenant Commander Chung Hua Li was a 17 year veteran in the People's Liberation Army Navy (PLAN). His current billet as the Senior Watch Officer at the PLAN Hainan Island Base was an assignment that he could not understand. He had risen quickly through the ranks, leaving his junior officer peers behind through **his** dedication, perseverance, **and even quite a bit of butt kissing**. He had done everything correctly; punched all the right tickets yet, look where it landed him. Instead of a advanced position on the staff of a senior Admiral in Peking or an advanced naval base with operational assets capable of deploying to meet western aggression, he wound up in Hainan! Hainan, a place where only those who were stationed there even knew where it was. As the smallest and southernmost province of the People's Republic of China, where was the upward mobility the party had promised him? Certainly not. Hainan, a place of relative obscurity located in the middle of nowhere. Never would he have a chance for the promotion he needed so badly. Without the promotion, he could never afford the tutoring needed for his dim-witted son to be accepted into a legitimate scientific university; never would he have enough money to shut his nagging wife's mouth; never, never, never!

He believed in the party to which he dedicated his life and adhered to its philosophies even when in direct conflict to his own. What had it gotten him? A senior watch officer assignment in Hainan!

The base commander, Captain Fong, provided the perfect example of what an officer in the Chinese, military, or any other military for that matter, should not be. Fong's peers regarded him as a fossil, one who the military was anxious to let live out his retirement years **in** relative obscurity; perhaps his best skill was pitting his officers against each other, putting assets likely loyalty and camaraderie completely aside. No one trusted anyone - the only skills developed by junior officers were slipping the knife in to and out of each other's back.

At least the island provided white sandy beaches and a multitude of beautiful women to occupy any sailor's time so no one complained too harshly. Returning to the base was **however,** much like crossing the line between heaven and the proverbial hot place!

LCDR Li knew that he must be extremely careful to be able to endure his tour of duty on **Hainan,** he must measure every word carefully and appear to continue to be the ass-kisser his comrades **thought he was**. At least the conscripts could enjoy their time in Hainan; they knew they were not going anywhere **anyway;** they could continue enjoying Colonel Fong destroy the spineless officer corps that surrounded him. Chung knew his only way out was to shift emphasis to himself; to create some type of attention to a present or near future accomplishment which would place him at the center of attention to those senior to Captain Fong. At the same time, however, it must not appear to be in conflict with any assignment the Captain made. He must not let the Captain lose face but, at the same time, substantiate Chung's importance to senior officers. Maybe, just maybe, this would result in a transfer and provide Chung an opportunity to excel and increase his upward mobility.

Chung continued to think. The reasons for transferring were obvious but, what, when, and how remained an enigma. He must also worry about Fong's response. Failure would mean further degradation even possible removal from the military. Captain Fong's history labeled him vengeful and Chung worried about what would happen to him and even his family should any conspiracy be concluded.

Chung would need help in the development of his plan. If only he could pull off some major focus to get him noticed at levels much higher than Fong. Then, perhaps, he could manage a transfer out of this God forsaken place and maybe, just maybe, a corresponding promotion to go with it. Lots of questions – what, when, and how and what would Fong's immediate reaction be? Thought processes abounded, preparation equaled success. Additionally, who could I seek as a co-conspirator? Who would have the intestinal fortitude to go against Fong and maintain secrecy in this miserable, no backbone wardroom? Whatever endeavor, it must happen while he was on duty and Fong was not present. This way, he could control the environment without threat of Fong's interference. Something operational – something that no one could suspect; something important enough so that he could cut Fong's throat when he would not even realize there was a knife present.

Chung needed to be most vigilant in scanning all of the operational messages, both incoming and outgoing. Anything that would appear even remotely possible to fill his requirements must be pursued, checked and double checked. He should be the responsible officer in the release of all messages to the PLAN. His initial thoughts were becoming part of his plan. If anything was suspected, he could always blame on being zealous in pursuit of his transfer. He must stress to pilots and air crews alike, the importance of his strict communications procedural compliance. These added pressures would serve a two-fold purpose – it could cause inept officers to make errors and satisfy questions of communications personnel in sending the type of messages he would release. Who would question his intentions while fearing his wrath if mistakes were made?

Chung was already feeling better as he thought out his intentions. He could see Fong attempting to explain situations to his superiors. He allowed himself a smile for the first time in months. Maybe he had this assignment all wrong; a gardener must prune to obtain the fruit of his labor!

The smile broadened - Fong stammering excuses while he would have all the answers.

"Yes sir the message came while Captain Fong was away"

"No sir, I did not know where Captain Fong was. I assumed he was in his quarters. I called his personal telephone but no one answered. Due to the serious nature of the communique, I called nearly every five minutes."

"No sir. I do not know who he was with. I assumed him to be alone."

Yes sir…I had command. I did what I thought was necessary, and might I say Sir, Captain Fong's confidence in me was…….."

The alarm went off. He woke and mumbled to himself I hope I don't talk in my sleep, Fong would kill me. Then he thought, do answers really come in dreams?

He smiled again.

Chapter Eleven

Just as the J-8II interceptor/fighter cleared the runway **and immediately went feet wet**, Lieutenant Chun broke into a broad smile. **The time between seeing the gray runway change to white sand, to aqua water, to light and then dark blue water passed in a heart beat.** How he loved to fly! What an airplane! The twin engine jet could cruise at 800 miles per hour with a combat radius of about 700 nautical miles and when he really wanted to punch it, it could obtain a top speed of about 1,450 miles per hour. Shenyang Aircraft, the plane's builder, really out did themselves even by Western standards.

Getting off the ground put him alone in another world; his only connection with the ground was the communications devices connected through the ear and microphones in his helmet. What phrase did the Americans use? - Something about touching the face of their God! He believed **that** every pilot **must feel** the euphoria associated with flying **when** the plane **once** left the earth. **While he lacked formal training, LT Chun volunteered for every mission; he had logged more hours than any other pilot of the PLAN on Hainan. While combat air patrol was out of the question, he practiced and studied every move of foreign**

pilots, particularly the Americans, until he perfected his movements. Through practice after practice he knew he was ready for anything the pilots of the rest of the world could throw against him.

Once the wheels were raised, he divorced himself from the pettiness and backstabbing associated with Captain Fong and the other pilots of the Air Wing. He looked to his left and watched his wingman assume his position next to him in a tight formation; even with his wingman there, Chun was alone. He thought of how, back home in Shanghai, there was no place to be alone, his environment would not allow it. He was a product of his environment; he was part of the Chinese way of life; sardines in a can. His small physical size made him a target. He **absorbed** many beatings and remembered vividly of crawling home, climbing hungry into his bed, and crying himself to sleep. There, he could dream of becoming a bird and flying far from Shanghai forever. To where? He did not care, just away from the life he lived – to soar alone, high in the heavens where white clouds could forever obscure the facts of his life. The daily beatings he endured may have beaten him up physically but they could not beat him down. Although physically lacking, he applied himself mentally, day-in and day-out and rose academically to the top of his class.

When he turned 18, his mental abilities and mathematical skills became legendary. A rich benefactor followed his young career with great interest and enrolled Chun in military school with promises of success in the future. His successes led to **limited** flight training **for China, at the time, had only a quasi-form of dedicated training and relied largely on acquiring their piloting**

skills from operational training. Despite this, his earlier thoughts of being a bird and flying away from Shanghai provided the impetus for dedication. Ironically, he owed the bullies of his youth a debt of gratitude for their actions were a direct cause for placing him in this current position.

Although he never had learned to totally shut out the world, he had mastered the technique of being one with the aircraft. Here in the clouds, it was just him and his plane - his passion. It was almost as if he could will the plane to do his bidding. Most other pilots fought the plane, trying to master the controls to do their bidding. LT Chun knew better. The way to maximize this aircraft was by subtle hints with rudder and throttle. Muscle control gently applied let the bird pull you into the fullness of the maneuver, the forces of machinery and gravity working in harmony, not against each other. It was the sheng-fei of flight. **He thought of it all and perfected his mindset and physical reactions.**

Without ever seemingly having to think, he throttled back at the precise altitude necessary to proceed on the first leg of his mission. While others dreaded the long hours of repetitive flight, he loved it.

This wonderful machine would serve him in a number of ways - first in its natural state, of course, a superb combat weapon; **but, as an alternative,** it would also serve as a springboard to freedom from all that was evil and distasteful in his life. By becoming the best pilot in the PLAN, he could wield another tool, political power. His skills would make Captain Fong take notice and then he and Fong could climb the ladder together. The other alternative would be to just fly away, Thailand or Taiwan were both possibilities and the F-8 would be his ticket out of China to the West - what a ticket, what a ride and above all, what a prize all in one package. The fools back in Hainan would probably not even notice he was gone until one of the mechanics noticed the plane was missing. Then Captain Fong would have heads for breakfast, lunch and dinner; he'd clean house at Hainan!!

The plane slipped through the air and in and out of the clouds, either way he would be free of those things which he had learned in life to be patient with, for Confucius himself said "The bird flies, but must have a nest. Yes where to nest would be the determining factor. **Would it be the** East or **the** West? He must sharpen his focus! He must be ready for he knew he would only get one opportunity and it must be soon,

Chapter Twelve

Sam Colby looked at the communication he received from his White House insider – interns had more than one use at 1600 Pennsylvania Ave. - involuntarily he shuddered. If the information was true, they had little time. Finding a suitable countermeasure would be next to impossible. Frequently he'd receive similar reports but each was missing significant parts which put it all together – and now here it was – how could he, once the cat was out of the bag.

He pressed the intercom to his secretary- Millie Devry

"Millie, get Logan on the line at once; call my wife and tell her I won't be home for dinner, then order Chinese – it's going to be a long night."

Since the damage would be catastrophic the remedy had to be as equally great or greater – it would be another one of these undefined moments in history when the decisions of a few profoundly affect the lives of everyone on the planet.

His phone rang, it was Logan.

"Evening Sam. Just a heads up! Senator Webster has dispatched a Special Investigative Team to FEMA. They are being empowered to look into every facet of FEMA's budget, including that unrelated to natural emergencies. I am sure you know what that means", explained Logan.

The Federal Emergency Management Agency was initiated during Nixon's administration in response to the cold war and the possibility of nuclear attack to ensure the survivability of the United States. Ensuing administrations, from Carter through Bush, continued to empower the agency through a series of Executive Orders. While the general public believed **then, and continues to believe today, that** FEMA's sole purpose is disaster preparedness and response, only about 6 percent of its budget is spent as such. The largest amount of FEMA's budget has been spent of the construction of secret underground facilities to assure the U.S. government can continue to run the country in the case of major emergencies; emergencies that could be caused by other than natural disasters. FEMA's charter also allowed the government to provide domestic intelligence and surveillance of U.S. citizens, restrict the movement of its citizens within the United States, allow the government to isolate large groups of citizens, use the National Guard to seal borders and control U.S. airspace and ports of entry. These powers obviously go a lot further than responding to natural disasters.

"Appreciate the follow-up and thanks for the information Logan. I sincerely appreciate your loyalty", replied Sam. He hung up the telephone.

Sam knew this day would come but **hoped it would not be at such an inopportune time such as now.** His mind raced rapidly playing scenario after scenario. Webster not now, He tried to recall any scrap of information that would help him stand under the scrutiny of Webster's inquisition. Like any good intel operative, he had committed to memory significant reasons that could be used to justify

FEMA actions. FEMA's creation in the '60's provided our government with an agency designed to circumvent red tape and apply solutions to problems with or without the benefit of congressional approval. Sam realized that taking over the agency could someday lay the blame for misappropriations at his doorstep, but loyalty to the United States substantiated this risk. He would be happy to accept "blame" as long as what he was being blamed for provided for the security of his country.

Chapter Thirteen

As anticipated, it did not take long for word to get out that the President was going to provide the Communist Chinese government and military with heretofore secret information regarding United States submarine and missile capabilities. How could he have done it? Better yet, how can he get away with it! The Constitution of the United States was designed to prevent situations just like this and had survived, as the United States had, for over two hundred years. The President, the President of the United States, was selling his own country out! What happened to the checks and balances designed into our government?>

LT Frank Christmas looked around and, in his mind, reviewed the service records of all his crew members. Their loyalty and devotion to duty was documented and vetted by various agencies of the government; their security clearances granted based on their background investigations. There was not a single member of the crew who didn't have a security clearance of the highest nature; equal to, and in some cases higher, than his. These clearance processes took years of investigation; the vetting process verified the importance of each and every person on his aircraft. His crew was young yet, to a man, he was positive of their loyalty to their country. He knew there was no way they would sell out their country, not matter what the offer. Where could you go and not be a pariah? He lifted his hear to God.

"Father – give me the strength to see this mission to its end. Give me strength my crew together, protect them, for in truth they do not know what I am about to do. Be with Mom and Dad, Lord, protect them from the blood lust of the Washington politicians and media and bring to naught all who conspire against you. I pray in Jesus name."

As he banked and started his preparations for the final leg of the 6-hour recon mission, his thoughts reviewed the beginning of the trip. The aircraft, an EP-3 Aries, who some called a "spy plane" because its mission included Electronics Intelligence (ELINT), was packed with highly technical collection, analysis, and recording equipment and manned by Cryptologic Technicians stationed at Fleet Reconnaissance Squadron One (VQ-1) in Okinawa.

His crew was a magnificent collection of technicians (referred to as "spooks" by other rates in the Navy) who tested the mastery of their job on a "live" basis every day and on every flight. **Much like their counterparts on the surface, subsurface, and ashore**, they drilled in every phase of their profession from technical data collection through the destruction of classified information in the event of possible compromise and/or capture by the enemy. Their on-site analysis of collected information provide immediate and direct support to the operations of air, surface and subsurface assets in any given operational area.

LT Christmas had total faith in his crew and their capabilities. They, too, had similar faith in their pilot.

"Mark, check the crew and make ready for final."

"Aye, Aye, Skipper!" replied his co-pilot.

Chapter Fourteen

In response to Senator Webster's tasking, Blair Jordan immediately immersed himself in the task.

Blair formed a plan on the run; he laid out the numbers of incoming and outgoing expenditures and compared them to government tasking requirements. After hours of perusing seemingly unending data sheets and adjusting data columns and lines with additional formulas, he realized something was wrong, very wrong. Things did not add-up and immediately he could not understand how these miscalculations could have escaped detection so long. It was obvious to him, after just minimal analysis, that the line item budget appropriations were never even cross checked! Indeed; who was providing oversight on this as well as other government projects concerning FEMA.

Blair knew he could trace things **back as** many years **as he wanted**, back as far as the mid 1950's when Hurricane Hazel caused widespread damage to the northeast. A quick scan indicated that each time FEMA issued funds for catastrophic recovery applications, the allocated monies were exceeded by approximately 8% of that which was requested. For an agency which routinely expended hundreds of millions, even billions of dollars, 8% added up pretty quickly! In accordance with his quick mental application, approximately $315 million dollars was unaccounted for. His findings were unbelievable and he had only scratched the surface. As was obvious, **it appeared** someone was lining their pockets with taxpayer's money. The Government Accounting Office (GAO) obviously did not recognize the fraud because it was right in front of their faces!

Now that he had identified this specific discrepancy and **he brashly** assumed additional investigations would uncover other "misrepresentations", Blair wanted to track the money train, identify the parties, and figure it out so that he could use it to his advantage. He knew Senator Webster would keep him around as long as it was to the Senator's advantage. Equally, if the Senator's career was damaged and his job threatened, would he survive? Webster made enemies quicker than Genghis Khan and his list of enemies was long; they would be quick to take advantage of any mud available.

Taking this investigation forward would have to be his most meticulous research ever. He would collect as much information as possible but he would only provide the Senator with as much as necessary to keep his boss happy (and curious). This could be his personal brass ring; the ring for which every politician had hoped. Now, he needed to ensure he could manipulate this treasure accordingly.

He would collate FEMA's expenditures over the last 5 years – then use GAO accounts as the first cross reference - he would then need the state and county expenses for each event. He would then cross check FEMA's expenses/salaries and supplemental requests over the same period. If there was a needle in this hay stack, he'd find it, then exploit it; carefully exploit it. Webster wouldn't grab this one out from under him, now he had a reason to research and not raise any suspicions.

Chapter Fifteen

Paul Webster seethed – If Jane Story thought she was going to have a free ride to the White House she was crazier than he thought she was, President's wife or not. **He would fight her every step of the way; he would present a formidable opponent to Mrs Story they day she decided to put her foot into the nasty world of the political ring he in which he was so experienced.**

The First Lady admittedly, had access to every piece of data, both founded and unfounded, rumor or truth, for her to secure the top seat on the next ticket. Her husband remained however, **the significant** albatross around her neck. Everyone knew her husband thought more often with his little head rather than the one on his shoulders. Sure, he chased every skirt that passed (and caught quite a few of them); it was common knowledge but yet, it was the elephant in the room that no one discussed. **Mrs. Story** had the public sympathy for "standing by her man" rather than succumbing to the pressures of his infidelities **while he was** in public office. Her abilities to, what was the Far Eastern phrase – save face for the country kept her in the voter's hearts, **and she remained as** one of the most **esteemed and respected First Lady's** since the likes of Jackie Kennedy and Nancy Reagan.

Webster **however,** knew that a few well-timed leaks about her escapades with union officers, in particular with Susan Green, credited to anonymous sources close to the First Lady would, in fact, lead to knocking her off the inside track. **This was the way of dirty politics.** Documenting her penchant for power and desire to totally socialize the country through her activist judge friends and the radical left should seal her doom. This was the United States and its citizens would never allow the government to control them across the board!

Timing again would be the key – first, he would announce progress on his current crusade. Then, through surreptitious press releases about "Mrs. President", he could claim she was diverting attention from his latest disclosure – the domino effect. The American public, as naïve as they were, would soon cast enough doubt on her to make it appear that the radical left was attempting to establish a stepping stone to launch a bid for the Presidency. Then he thought – is it worth it? I mean the prize would alone be anti-climactic – but the game was what it was all about –the prize would be totally acceptable but then the living of it every day would be the extreme. Maybe the senator was the mark. Money too – how could he possibly raise enough money – there was much, much more to think about –but not now, things were starting to turn sour – time for a break. He couldn't keep it all on track right now. Maybe it was a "small" "big" something relatively insignificant on the surface, but huge in the light of a full intense inquiry time would tell, it always did.

Chapter Sixteen

A twidget; in the Navy, is a term of affection foisted on those who performed any of a series of technical jobs such as Cryptologic Technicians or Electronics Technicians, the jobs have restricted access due to their associated sensitivities.

There were literally thousands of twidgets, one of whom was Petty Officer First Class John Prescott, known as "JJ".

"JJ" was a SQUALL analyst. **Being** a Navy enlisted man, the company developing SQUALL was able to take advantage of his technical and analytical abilities at a fraction of the cost required for that of his civilian counterparts. **This occurred all the time in the contract world, even in the government. A few of JJ's shipmates spent time at NSA working the same analytical problems next to the desks of civilian employees making many times his salary while performing the same functions. The wage difference was always there but hardly ever discussed. Most military people just looked forward to retiring and getting the "big bucks". This time, h**is primary function was to study and the analyze SQUALL Targeting Systems for the Navy to allow our forces **to locate, identify, track, and** prosecute enemy targets and initiate countermeasures to render their operational electronics less effective.

JJ's ten years of naval service and training provided him with the technical know-how to exploit the enemy's electronics and communications in ways their designers never thought possible. **Unfortunately however,** throughout his efforts, he **understood** that the SQUALL technology would **somehow, despite all efforts to safeguard the classified information,** end up in the hands of those who would try and use it against the United States. Look at the USS PUEBLO back in the 1960s – the North Koreans captured the ship nearly intact **with an unknown amount of the** classified equipment and information for their own analysis and subsequent exploitation and countermeasures **by the Soviet Union and China. How much classified information was provided to our enemies by the John Walker spy ring from the 1960's through the 1980's? We would never really know but it changed the face of naval and air warfare strategies conducted by our Navy just as SQUALL would change warfare as we know it today. As such, it had to be given the highest security protection possible!**

Working with Ernesto Sharp, his civilian counterpart, Petty Officer Prescott's efforts provided the impetus for the discovery, although accidental, of the Achilles Heel of the system. If not programmed exactly, a system generated virus could slowly work its way through the system and render SQUALL as less than reliable. What was difficult to understand was that only he and Ernesto seemed aware of this anomaly; their contemporaries seemed to have no knowledge. JJ labeled his discovery "Barnacle" a nautical term for a nautical system. But in fact, a barnacle was something that attached itself to a host then grows and multiplies until it impedes its host's ability to function properly. How appropriate. Like most computer viruses, SQUALL would appear to work but after time would give false readings making target prosecution all but futile. If incorporated within command, control, computers, and communications scenarios, it would become the "barnacle", and over time it would produce calculable results - a definite advantage for the **United States. Had he and Ernesto inadvertently created the ultimate discovery – an undiscoverable security system within a massive command, control, and communications (C3) system that, if compromised, would destroy the computer systems of the enemy when launched in their C3 capacity?**

JJ thought of terminating his naval service and attempting to go for the big bucks with his discovery. After all, civilians sitting right next to him were making quadruple the money he was being paid and, of course, he wanted a bigger piece of the pie. But, his discovery was actually accidental and his devotion to serving his country outweighed personal gain.

Although unusual for a person of his rank, Petty Officer Prescott asked his senior officers and contemporaries, both military and civilian, to hold a technical discussion to outline his discoveries. He explained the situation, delving into the intricacies of the virus and his findings. Impact was, literally, immediate.

After hours of explanation and acceptance of the vulnerability, real-time SQUALL operations were immediately suspended pending the findings of a special technical board of review. Within weeks, the Navy and NSA (The National Security Agency) and Naval Weapons

Systems Command evaluated and analyzed the situation and produced an effective Barnacle anti-virus. Its classification was higher than the classification of the system it served to preserve its functionality. The United States now was capable of correcting an anomaly in its own system without the same system being suspected of a deficiency! Should the SQUALL system fall into enemy hands and then be exploited without the anti-virus it would quickly render their command, control, computer, and communications systems useless.

JJ thought of how dangerous things would be if the scenario involving the incorporation of the virus were known even in the tightest of circles. Our enemies command and control would be compromised and jeopardized into complete and utter failure. As such, the U.S. would have no equal and peace would be sustained on our terms.

Chapter Seventeen

The initial leg of their flight was somewhat boring as the crew did not engage in operational activities until arrival on-station. Once on-station, it was all business as each crew member relied on the others to ensure their safety and eventual return to base. The transit time allowed Frank to think back and relive the last month of flight preparation and briefings.

Eight officers (including LT Christmas) of the Reconnaissance Squadron on Okinawa were being flown back to the Washington, DC area for briefings with high level officials concerning upcoming air maritime patrols near the Chinese coast; four pilots and four cryptologic officers. None of the eight were provided explanations for this highly unusual move; they were only directed to arrive at the National Security Agency at 0900 on the morning following their arrival in the states.

It was now that time and all the officers, following security identification procedures on entry to NSA, were assembled in a typical government large briefing room with state-of-the-art briefing capabilities. Even now, none of the eight in the room was aware of why they were here.

The reason unfolded quickly.

Concurrent with the opening of the door at the front of the conference room, "Attention on deck!" was sounded loudly and clearly, followed by the entry of more brass than Frank has seen congregated in one room in his entire time in the Navy. A full Navy Captain assumed a position behind the podium.

"Ladies and gentlemen, due to the classification level and compartmentalization classifications of today's briefing, you will all be required to read and sign Non-Disclosure Agreements (NDA) concerning the information of which you are about to be briefed and discussion of information surrounding its implementation. Under no circumstances will this information be discussed in other than appropriately cleared spaces and with appropriately cleared personnel. Is that understood?"

All heads nodded affirmatively around the table as the NDAs were passed out.

The Captain continued, "Please read the three-page document and place your signature in the indicated space and date the document with today's date. **Please note, with special care, the penalties involved in the event of the inadvertent or advertent disclosure of the information about to be discussed. There will be no exceptions to the rules gentlemen!** Petty Officer LaMarr will collect the documents and file them accordingly. Thank you."

Each of the eight squadron officers read the NDAs line by line with a few eyebrows being raised during their reviews.

The Captain continued. "Ladies and gentlemen the classification of this briefing is TOP SECRET Limited Distribution (LIMDIS) and concerns the operation of the

SQUALL submarine and missile detection countermeasures system currently installed aboard two EP-3E aircraft being operated by Reconnaissance Squadron (VQ-1) based in Okinawa."

The squadron officers glanced at one another while the cryptologic officers appeared to be aware of exactly what the Captain was about to brief.

"Please be advised that any notes taken during the briefing will be classified TOP SECRET and serialized for forwarding via courier to your command. At no time will these notes be referred to, studied, or discussed outside of squadron special intelligence spaces. Any discussions concerning the information to be briefed will only be conducted with those personnel in-briefed to the current program entitled BARNACLE."

The briefer continued. . . . "You are fully aware of the capabilities of the SQUALL system. You have seen it operate and have used the information gleaned from its SIGINT and ELINT information gathering. SQUALL provides us the capability to detect and track enemy submarines and missile systems for their ultimate targeting and destruction. What you don't is that our analysts, both civilian and military alike have discovered a flaw in the system that, when uncontrolled, injects a virus which generally renders the system useless by throwing off both operational and targeting information,"

The cryptologic officers in the group began whispering to each other in their true behind the green door attitude. Tradition had always placed the crypto guys and the technicians separate from the crew with the infamous green door to their spaces controlling access.

"Gentlemen, please. There will be a time for discussion upon conclusion of the brief."

"The most important part of this virus discovery is that it can be controlled and we, both NSA and the Navy, have exploited this virus and will profit by its ability to alter the Command and Control efforts and capabilities of our enemies."

This statement got the attention of every individual in the room.

Without being recognized, Chief Warrant Officer **Bob** Cutler, Frank's normal **cryptologic** crew member, blurted out, "Captain, we have a virus in SQUALL, how do we get it to the enemies Command and Control system?"

"That is exactly where you all come in", explained the Captain. "You all are aware of the harassment tactics being used by the Chinese PLAN during our reconnaissance mission over the East China Sea area. Due to Chinese air belligerence, we have come extremely close to air-air collisions on numerous occasions. In essence, what we are hoping is that one of these incidents will cause enough problems to force an EP-3E to land intact on Chinese soil."

"WHAT", Frank called out. "Captain, are you telling us to purposely endanger our aircraft and crew to land our plane at a CHICOM airfield and allow our plane to be compromised?"

The Admiral sitting in the first row turned his chair around to look at Frank. "Lieutenant, you are half wrong and half right. We do not want you to endanger your crew, we want you to take advantage of any situation or incident that the CHICOMS may cause in the future. If, and I stress the word IF, such a situation arises, and we can land one of our planes on their soil, we must take advantage of that situation; let them think they are successful with their harassment. Once the EP-3E is on the ground, the Chinese technicians will obviously go through the aircraft with a fine-toothed comb and copy/steal anything worth stealing, including SQUALL."

"With all due respect Admiral," **Cutler blurted out** "what idiot dreamt this project up?"

The Admiral responded, "With the exception of your squadron **and many of your senior cryptologic whizzes**, all the idiots sitting in this room! Let us continue."

"To re-emphasize, should the situation arise", continued the Captain, "your abilities as pilots and officers will be tested completely. The CHICOMS will probably not initially accept your credibility; it will be up to you to convince them of your credibility. We realize this is a long shot and is totally dependent upon a given situation. Again, if that situation arises, we must take advantage of it."

Chapter Eighteen

As the EP-3E began its approach to their planned operations area, Frank banked the aircraft slightly to starboard to bring him into approach to their flight plan over the East China Sea.

Frank once again thought of the briefing and preparation for their ongoing mission. Four reconnaissance flights had taken place since their flight to Washington and back with little or no Chinese interference. Now that they had a plan, no Chinese interaction was occurring. Isn't that the way it always happens?

As if someone was reading his mind, Frank's radar intercept operator in the rear of the aircraft squawked him on internal communications, "Skipper, I have two unidentified and potentially hostile aircraft approaching from 270 degrees with their air search radars active. ETA approximately two minutes."

"Roger approaching aircraft", Frank acknowledged.

"Mark, keep your eyes out for the bogeys and let me know of a visual ID", he instructed his co-pilot.

"Roger."

"Captain, I have fire control radars active in their acquisition mode emanating from the unidentified aircraft. Radars fit into the parameters of the Chinese PLAN."

Frank knew this was normal procedure for military aircraft; a 'lock-on" would however, violate international agreements and satisfy the first rule of engagement for retaliation by his plane. Frank rolled the aircraft slightly to port to change course and see if the bogeys followed suite.

The radar intercept operator punched his mike once again, "Sir, intermittent fire control lock-ons. The definitely know we are here! **We cannot identify to fire control radar.""**

His co-pilot piped in, "Skipper, two bogeys visual. Looks like two J-8 II's of the Chinese PLAN at 180 degrees. Coming in fast!"

LT Christmas watched closely as the J-8 jet passed close by the P-3. He glanced to his right to address his co-pilot.

"Mark, communicate our altitude and position to home base immediately. Altitude 22,000 feet, speed 180 knots, heading 110 degrees. Our current position is about 100 miles from Hainan Island."

"Let Okinawa know that we have two, repeat two, J-8 PLAN aircraft flanking our current position; intentions unknown. They have us hemmed in and are apparently are having difficulty slowing to our speed. The Chinese are attempting to alter our course. Prepare comms for emergency transmission transmission to CINCPACFLT, CNO, and the White House!"

Frank thought, "Be careful what you wish for" as both Chinese aircraft peeled off for a re-approach from their tail.

As the co-pilot/navigator commenced the position reporting, the same J-8 passed closed aboard for the second time. As suspected, the jets were having a tough time slowing to their airspeed. Frank noticed the pilot hand-signaling him to follow **by first pointing at the P-3 then to himself and then to a course to his right.**

Frank went to internal communications. "**Warrant, you and the Chief**, prepare to initiate emergency destruction on my command."

The crew in the rear of the P-3 immediately began loading various manuals and documents into weighted bags. All classified material was printed on water soluble paper to ensure that once in contact with the ocean below, the paper would dissolve into indiscernible mush. The technicians moved automatically as they had been trained for years in the emergency destruction techniques they were about to initiate. Physical destruction of all classified equipment would be incurred with fire axes and sledge hammers. **This was not something new as it had happened many times when they were harassed by the Chinese on other flights. Load up the bags and just unload them later and put everything back in the shelves. This time, like others, could be the real thing however, so each of the crewmembers treated it as such.**

Frank knew that P-3 flights similar to his had been harassed by the Chinese for the past couple of months. Military experts had expressed that previous P-3 missions were deliberately endangered by Chinese PLAN jets. CINCPACFLT supported the experts by communicating to the free world press that the intercepts were endangering both the Chinese and Americans.

'No **shit**", he thought. Now Frank was sitting in the hot seat but known only to him and Cutler, this time with a purpose.

The Chinese jet again approached on the port side of the P-3. **The Chinese pilot was doing everything he could to lower his speed to match that of the P-3 but in doing so, his aircraft was swaying back and forth while trying to maintain headway.**

BOOOOM!!!! The Orion shuddered violently and banked hard to the left as the J-8 collided with **the port wing** of the U.S. aircraft. Frank used all of his strength to counter the impact; instrumentation was already going bananas. **The P-3 banked to the left and went in to an immediate dive.**

"Mark, send the **CRITIC** message. Ensure our position is correct!" Initiate a MAYDAY. We are going down!"

"Chief **Edwards**, initiate emergency destruction; jettison the material and destroy all the cryptographic equipment! Get everyone prepared to bail out!"

Frank immediately attempted to assess damage while fighting for control of the aircraft. The J-8 had broken into two pieces and Frank watched momentarily fascinated as the wing of the jet spirally parasailed towards the sea - no parachutes deployed. The P-3's outboard propeller was damaged severely which was contributing to the loss of speed and altitude. He was unaware that the J-8's tail fin was stuck in the left aileron which was causing the P-3 to roll to port. His arms ached from trying to pull the plane out of an almost uncontrollable dive.

The P-3 was in a 30 degree dive and almost upside down. The aircraft had lost nearly 14,000 feet in altitude before Frank finally regained control. His only option, other than a water landing, was the possibility of conducting an emergency landing on Hainan Island.

"Chief, what is the status of emergency destruction?"

"Sir, we are continuing to jettison the bags and destroy equipment. All crew members are prepared to debark the aircraft on your command." **"Be advised that Follow-up CRITICs are being issued accordingly."**

"Roger, stand-by Chief!"

Frank was going to make every attempt to save the crew and, if possible, the aircraft. His only real option was a landing at Lingshui airfield on Hainan Island. Sort of ironic, Hainan Island was the site of a Chinese signals intelligence facility that tracked U.S. activities in the South China Sea and was the target off collection efforts of the P-3 crew. Now, Frank was about to attempt an emergency landing attempt on the same island.

For approximately 30 minutes, LT Christmas wrestled with the controls of the P-3. Distress signals continued to be automatically transmitted at approximate one minute intervals. Both the U.S. and Chinese governments were obviously aware of his predicament but there had been no communications whatsoever. Probably who ever acknowledged the situation first would lose face.

CRITIC messages being sent by the cryptologic contingent aboard the aircraft were being transmitted and received to/by the President of the United States, appropriate members in the strategic chain of command as well as the Commander in Chief of the Pacific Fleet (CINCPACFLT) and those in the tactical chain of command. Like many operations involving cryptologic

equipped ships or aircraft, these units operated without benefit of any supporting combat equipped units and were virtually on their own. Such was the case of LT Christmas' aircraft -there was no U.S. forces close enough to render immediate aid.

Thoughts raced through Frank's mind. Landing the aircraft in Chinese territory would obviously result in capture of his crew and any remaining classified information. This would result in review after repeated review of the incident. The captain of the USS Pueblo was dragged over the coals for years for surrendering his crew to the North Koreans. Frank knew his actions would have a similar result. The Chinese would claim the incident was the result of his aircraft's aggression or cross into Chinese airspace. Conversely, he and his crew, as long as they remained alive, would produce facts that the J-8 pilot deliberately maneuvered in to a collision with the Orion. Frank and his crew were currently alive; the J-8 pilot had most likely perished when his jet crashed in to the sea.

"Chief **Edwards**, we are going to make every attempt to land the aircraft safely on Hainan Island. Prepare the crew."

"WHAT! Are you kidding me? replied the Chief.

"You heard what I said. I want everybody strapped in for a hard landing. I want you to remind everyone quickly of their responsibilities under the Geneva Convention and the requirement to provide only name, rank, and serial number. Tell them all to hold out as long as possible. Try to take care of each other as long as possible. We are going to be in for a rough time **for possibly a long time**."

"Yes sir! Don't worry about us. You take care of the zeros... eh, officers and we will do whatever is required", replied the Chief.

The P-3 shuddered again. LT Christmas knew that the classified paperwork had been jettisoned and undoubtedly destroyed in the water. The cryptographic equipment was smashed beyond recognition. Mark had destroyed all the cryptographic codes on the flight deck. Frank was also aware that SQUALL could not be destroyed without the use of thermite so it would probably remain intact and be compromised.

As Frank continued to wrestle with the controls, Chinese air traffic controllers, using the international frequency, finally contacted the P-3.

"American aircraft, approach south to north using runway 4W. Wind speed is 8-10 east to west. When landing is complete, remain in the aircraft. Do not make any attempt to disembark; any attempt to leave aircraft will result in those people being shot. You will be met be representatives of the People's Liberation Army Navy and follow their instructions to the letter.

"Roger Hainan. **This is an emergency landing, will comply to the best of my ability. Request emergency vehicles be present at landing site.**" Frank replied. "No one will attempt to leave the plane until directed.

Although LT Christmas was unaware of his airspeed, he approached the runway as directed.

The Chinese arir controller repeated his instructions concerning the approach from south to north and acknowledged the emergency landing situation. "American aircraft, I repeat, NO ONE WILL MAKE

ANY ATTEMPT TO DISEMBARK THE AIRCRAFT THE AIRCRAFT UNTIL DIRECTED TO DO SO!"

"Chief, we are going in. All crew members assume crash position!"

"Mark. Lower the wheels!"

"Roger skipper"

"Chief, report" –

"Roger, Hainan Control. Will comply with your directions. Once on the ground, all personnel on board will remain on the aircraft until further advised. Please ensure emergency vehicles are prepared to treat casualties!"

"Roger, all NAVAIDS deep-sixed, all instructions, reports and messages – deep-sixed - all CRYPTO gear smashed." Frank waited. Then he heard it.

"SQUALL........

Chapter Nineteen

Flash precedence traffic always created a furor in any communications center and that of the Commander Naval Forces Japan was no exception. The EP-3E situation in the South China Sea now commanded everyone's attention. All forces were aware that the White House would be receiving the same message at the same time (just later in the day due to the time difference). The President of the United States was reading this message at the very same instance.

The operational deployment of U.S. Navy maritime and air assets would immediately be altered in response to the current situation. Jets were currently being scrambled at airfields in Japan and on Okinawa. The **USS ENTERPRISE** and its escorts and support ships, currently deployed in the Indian Ocean were ordered to proceed on an easterly course at maximum speed to assume positions in international waters to support any military action against China or the evacuation of military members from Hainan Island.

China was also preparing for the U.S. response although the type of which was currently unknown. Forces in southern China and Hainan Island were put on immediate alert. Naval assets were being deployed in defensive positions for monitoring U.S. forces and responding in full as required.

The Chinese news agencies Xinhua and the Chinese News Service had already initiated reporting of the latest atrocities of the United States Navy condemning their shoot down of the J-8 fighter plane operating in international waters approximately 100 nautical miles west of Hainan Island. They praised the actions of LT Chun, proclaiming him a posthumous hero for fighting against the western aggressors. With propaganda their best asset, the news services had already begun showing video of Chinese military might throughout the country.

Hainan Airfield was at full alert and had been for about 90 minutes. In response to national tasking from Peking, pilots had been scrambled and defense positions were manned; defense surface-to-air missile systems were activated. **While unconfirmed by U.S. intelligence sources, the Hainan PLAN forces were thought to have obtained the HQ-9 advanced intermediate long-range surface-to-air missile system from the Soviets yet intercepts by the P-3 could not confirm their existence; this had been one of their mission's primary objectives – to detect the HQ-9 systems. Such an existence would have alerted the P-3's profile with a lock-on capability out to at least 100 nautical miles. The Chinese could have brought the P-3 down nearly 1 hour ago without benefit of the jet aircraft however, they were their worst enemy - operation of these missile intercept capabilities were kept on a strict need-to-know and their use extremely limited.**

Initial rumors had a PLAN J-8 fighter being shot down by the Americans over the South China Sea. Follow-on reports indicated the PLAN aircraft was rammed in mid-air by an aggressive American pilot and resulted in the crash of the Chinese plane and the death of its pilot. About 90 percent of the base was unaware of the truth; only these deep within the Operations Center knew **a smattering of** the facts.

The loudspeaker within the Operations Center emitted a loud squawk.

"Comrades, may I have your attention. This is Captain Fong speaking. Another glorious day in the history of the People's Liberation Army Navy is underway. Your **comrades** have succeeded in intercepting an American aircraft, which was violating Chinese airspace, and have forced the aircraft to make a landing at our airfield here on Hainan Island, on **OUR ISLAND.**" The Captain paused **for effect.**

"We must all pause to pay our respects to LT Chun, the pilot of our interceptor, who lost his life when the pilot of the American aircraft deliberately caused a mid-air collision without provocation in the American's **futile attempt to out maneuver our superior pilot and** flee the area. LT Chun's actions and loyalty to you and our country are unprecedented and he will surely go down in history as a most revered hero", he continued.

Cheers rose from those manning the Operations Center.

Now that Captain Fong has fed their egos, he must also put a damper on their communications. "Although today is a glorious day and a time for reflection and celebration, we must not compromise our position and information to those foreign governments who seek our demise. Therefore, today's actions and future repercussions must remain classified at the highest levels and will not be discussed outside the Operations Center."

"The American aircraft, although damaged, has been grounded largely intact **and is currently surrounded by our troops at the airfield. The American plane is a P-3 spy plane and is incapable of further flight.** Further information will be promulgated on an as needed basis."

Now came the political posturing and excuse making. Captain Fong knew the Chinese government would assume the position of victim in the eyes of the world. Regardless of the truth, the Americans were spying on China and, by virtue of their guilt, make all attempts to flee the area and project to the world that they were in international airspace. This attempt to flee resulted in the collision with the Chinese jet and the death of the Chinese pilot.

With the American plane on the ground, detention of the crew and their isolation from the rest of the world was paramount. Orders from above were coming hot and furious. No one, repeat no one, would have access to the American crew without higher approval. An interrogation team was being assembled and flown from Peking; they would arrive within 24 hours. All international news was to be blacked out; of course, **every American news station would be requesting access to Hainan Island and the military compound immediately.** The future was now and none too soon.

Captain Fong smiled inwardly. His name would be on the lips of every major party member **and every American news reporter** for days, weeks, even months. With a coup such as this, he dared think of the future Admiral Fong!

He signaled for his Intelligence Officer, Major Chow Fat. The Major snapped to immediate attention. "Yes Sir!"

Captain Fong said, "We've a special mission from HQ – bring me all information on the American Orion aircraft – and I mean EVERYTHING!. Once the American crew is removed, our technicians will dismantle the aircraft piece by piece. Particular emphasis is to be placed on all computer equipment. I want every hard drive copied and any equipment that is not readily available on the open market inventoried, photographed, and documented. Operator manuals should be cataloged and studied for further operational characteristics."

He'd have this little onion peeled and plated before anyone could say "Chairman Mao" 3 times fast.

Major Fat got the feeling his life was no longer his own! "Right away Captain, right away."

Captain Fong was not going to wait for instructions from Peking. He did not need any. He had been around long enough to know what to do without direction. Yes, even in the Chinese PLAN, some of the senior officers had the common sense to make a move when such a move was necessary. He would stay a step ahead of the old men who sat in the stuffy little offices in Peking while he remained at an operational command. He had approximately7 24 hours to dissect the aircraft and prepare for the arrival of the senior people from the capital. They would, indeed, be surprised when he had already taken the initial **and follow-up** steps to establish some working knowledge of the equipment on the American aircraft.

***"Yes sir, Admiral Fong, your table in Peking will be ready in a moment"*, he dreamed confidently.**

Chapter Twenty

Logan Arnold hesitated at the door of the Oval Office. The Chief of Staff had, on numerous occasions, caught the President in various compromising positions when walking through the door unannounced. This time, he did not care. He turned the knob and walked in.

President Story was sitting behind the desk with his eyes closed and back arched; he attempted to stand up immediately. As he stood, he knocked the intern on her back. His pants were unbuttoned and almost fell to his knees. If the urgency of the matter was any less, it would be a great X-rated video comedy.

"What the.....", he screamed!

Why was it that every time Logan needed to report something to him, the President was engaging in some type of non-presidential activity? It seemed that the President of the United States would be better suited for the adult movie industry!

"Excuse me Mr. President, there is an urgent . . . . . .

The President interrupted Logan in mid-sentence. "How many times have I told you to knock before entering", he yelled while attempting to collect himself.

He looked at the girl. "Get up and get out here!"

"So what is it this time?"

"Sir, a U.S. Navy Orion has collided with a Chinese fighter over the South China Sea and has attempted to make an emergency landing in Hainan. As far as we know, the crew is safe and no one was injured. It's also believed a Chinese fighter went down – no word on status of the Chinese."

"Well that is just wonderful – now what? Can't the military do anything right? That's all I need – OK, meet me in the situation room in ten minutes, no press. Get me the Senate and House leaders and the Joint Chiefs - who's my Chinese expert? Whoever it is, get them, too. Have the media sit on this until I give them the OK, and then write me a press release. Tell them we're taking appropriate action; investigation, we're not sure what type of retribution the Chinese expect – we regret the whole incident... oh and that we're looking into courts martial options – no make that possible – no even better – it is too early to contemplate courts martial options just yet; and, keep Mrs. Story outta here."

"Yes sir", replied his Chief of Staff. Logan was amazed at his ability to be on the receiving end of an illicit act and change in to the Commander-in-Chief of the most technologically advanced military in the world in a matter of seconds. Logan left the room.

The President sat back down at his desk and thought. Now, how could be turn this idiotic military blunder to his advantage.

After a few minutes, he picked up the red phone and dialed Hua's personal number. If he played his cards right, he might come out of this looking like a genius – even

Presidential. Now, where did he park that young intern? He was feeling even more amorous than before.

The media imbeciles would sing whatever tune he wanted them to and the lovely lady Jane, she'd do anything to go from being the First Lady to becoming the President.

Oh, how he loved being President! Hua, listen here good buddy, I understand you have one of our aircraft over there on some tiny little island, Is that right? That's right a spy plane, what'd ya think, it was the granddaddy of all storks. Hua stammered something unintelligible. Story thought the media dopes would sing whatever song he wanted them to. The lovely Lady Jane, she'd do anything to become **President** Jane, He chuckled to himself when he thought of her in charge. In just a few short weeks, she would have the resignations of every top officer in the U.S. Military. Next, in order to pay off all of her political debt, she'd scale the military down to bare bones, redirecting funds to where they were really needed. In just a few months she would do more damage to the U.S than all of the worlds armies combined; and she would do it blaming all of the opposition parties – misogynist, Mrs. Misters.

Chapter Twenty-One

LT Christmas fought the aircraft as much as possible; his reputation as being the best pilot in the squadron would be substantiated when the entire incident was reviewed. He had little left when the wheels of the P-3 finally touched terra firma. He struggled with the aircraft as it bounced down the runaway, careening from side to side. He reversed throttle on what little engines he had left and applied the brakes with both feet while never letting go of the yoke. He could already see the movement of military and rescue vehicles **with their red lights blinking** along the runway. Of particular note were the troop carriers brimming with armed soldiers.

The aircraft finally skidded to a halt, **dragging its port wing,** with only a limited amount of runway remaining.

"We're here", Frank said to his co-pilot.

"Don't know if that is good or bad", replied LTJG Salerno **sarcastically.** "At least it is dry but those armed troops don't look like **much of** a welcoming party."

"Chief: status".

"About 75 percent of the printed material was jettisoned; most cryptographic keys and equipment **was** destroyed. Doubt if anyone could get anything useful from the **equipment of the** communications guys. L T, we could not completely destroy SQUALLS. When the Chicoms get in here, it will, **without a doubt,** be compromised. If and when we get out of here, we need to bring the inability to destroy SQUALLS back to the attention of the powers to be."

"Roger, Chief. Just get the word out for everybody to cooperate as best they can without revealing anything classified. Do the best you can once the Chicoms get aboard and it hits the fan. **We are on the ground safe, I don't want the Chicoms doing anything to injure the crew. Tell the troops not to try and act like heros either. They are undoubtedly going to separate the officers and enlisted – seems like something like this always happens. You keep things squared away like I know you will."**

"Aye Aye, Sir!

"Warrant", Frank queried, "what kind of status reporting have we gotten back to PACFLT and DC? Have the CRITIC follow-ups continued?"

"Roger Lieutenant". They know we are on the ground but at this point all communications are being jammed. We have received no confirmation from any of our chain of command that they have received any reports of our status!"

Frank thought back – how is it that things work the way they do? Here he was about to test every ounce of nerve and resilience he and his crew could muster but only he and his cryppie officer knew the truth. If he were alone it wouldn't be so bad, but, the crew! What would the crew think when the found out that they were actually patsies for the capture and compromise of one of the most advanced anti-submarines and anti-missile systems of the world. While a lot of lives were at stake, there were necessary to make the whole effort plausible. Frank did not know how long this would last. It could be days or, like the USS PUEBLO, it could last for months, even years. The crew would, most likely, be interrogated until the Chinese were satisfied with the answers. Interrogation techniques remained unknown.

Sam was right, however. The captured plane and its entire crew made it all believable. He and his staff had worked out everything with NSA; all the details. All he had to do was fly the airplane and take advantage of any opportunity that presented itself. Obviously, this opportunity was better than they could have predicted. The Chinese actually opened the door themselves! **In his heart, he felt as though he was betraying his fellow officers and his enlisted crew by knowing the things he knew and not being able to share the information with them. In the long run, it was probably better but, it weighed on his mind greatly.**

Intestinal fortitude! There was not going to be time to worry or even think for that matter. Frank, in particular, needed to settle in, be in control, and, most importantly, to sell the entire issue. The first parts of his mission **were** complete; he flew the plane, landed it, and provided the communists with a battered but still working SQUALL system.

He realized that pulling this off was a long shot but at the rate the Chinese were obtaining advanced technical data from rogue U.S. corporations, with the tacit blessing of the White House, there was no choice but to pursue this daring plan to its end, and even then – would it be enough? He remembered Sam and Katie when they told him that "all things were possible"... He let himself drift into that one thought - "ALL THINGS WERE POSSIBLE!".

Yea, well, we will see!

Chapter Twenty-Two

Petty Officer 1st Class Jonathan John Prescott (JJ) was the senior Petty Officer onboard the aircraft which entitled him as the LPO (Leading Petty Officer). In the pecking order, he fell right below the Chief but above all the other enlisted personnel on board. The Chief would tell him what was needed and he would ensure the orders were followed and carried out.

JJ could not remember ever wanting to do anything else in the Navy. The recruiter suggested he try the ET rating after achieving very high test scores in both the communications and computer segments. With his basic knowledge, he opted for CT school and quickly the basic school in Bainbrige, Maryland and picked up an additional 8 weeks of advanced training. His first duty station was Rota, Spain where he flew in both EA-3 and EP-3 Aries aircraft. Now, years later and after a tour at the funny farm at Fort Meade, he was a critical member of VQ-1 flying missions on the Orion.

JJ was a lifer. He thought of getting out of the Navy during his tour at NSA but common sense prevailed. Where else could he couple his experience with communications and computers with that of flying in some of the best aircraft the Navy could muster. His reputation was solid; he earned his Enlisted Aviation Warfare Specialist wings as quickly as he was able; his biggest hold up was the field time requirement. His chest was already filled with air and deployment medals. He would do this job for free! Next goal was the hat of a Chief Petty Officer. He had heard plenty of stories and rumors concerning getting initiated but he, and the many others before him, looked forward to that day.

JJ's technical career as a technician was without fault. His last tour at the agency earned him a Joint Service Commendation. Particularly, he had found a glitch in the computer system and provided guidance for using it to the Navy's advantage, the same system deployed on the aircraft on which he was aboard.

He could not even guess what his next step would be; maybe Chief Warrant Officer or Limited Duty Officer. Promotion to either officer rank would probably end his flying days. Promotion to the officer ranks would also provide the impetus for getting married. With more money; the greater chances of succeeding in sharing the rest of his life with Connie. She wanted to get married now but he did not relish the constant separations; he'd seen enough military marriages fail as a direct result of the husbands and wives being apart from one another. His dream promotions were still a year or two down the road. He would like to fly Connie out of Tokyo and meet her in Hong Kong where he would do the "down on one knee" thing.

He set SQUALL for what he knew would probably be its last mission; a command never given. He glanced at Phil and Clive; they were married and had a few curtain climbers. How did they do it? He knew Clive was one of those Christians but he was cool about it – he'd never heard of anyone being thumped with a Bible or anything – probably that was good for a married couple. He made a mental note to tell Clive when he'd got an OK from Connie. Yeah – married, wife, church; hey – he was becoming Mr. Model America – Cool! He remembered a book "God is My Co-Pilot if 'zeros" needed God he figured he would too.

His immediate priority was however, to survive his imminent capture by the Chinese Communists. They were going to be his immediate and major roadblock in realizing his dreams. He must first, get off the tarmac while he was still breathing. **God could be a great help to all of them right now!**

Chapter Twenty-Three

President Ernest Bradley (EB) Story finally completed his rendezvous with the smoking hot intern and turned his attention to the country's current dilemma. He patted "what's her face" on her pert little behind and let her relish in the fact she could brag to her girlfriends what she had done for the most powerful man in the world,

As he sat in the Oval Office, he sometimes had to pinch himself over his good fortune. He realized that his presidency was going more than the three or four levels deep behind the scenes where he had to go to pull strings to ensure his plans were successful. No great thinker was he; no great international statesman – his need for money unconditionally outweighed any sense of loyalty on his part. He would secretly become a billionaire right under everyone's noses.

The shallow and supercilious press, the power hungry party elite and the corporate greed mongers – he would use them all. By the time they figured it out, he'd be gone and beyond the reach of U.S. law. He would become one of them who made him. The immediate problem – find a way to keep everyone's attention focused around him but not on him. He would, right under their pompous noses, wheel and deal away while they would try to analyze his political good fortunes. Lots of luck! He had decided long ago that the greatest stage on earth was the United States of America and the greatest prop was Washington, D.C.

The greatest play on earth was acted out daily. Republicans and Democrats were each the antagonist and protagonist. How perfect – third party independents were pawns as were the press and political pundits' PACs and the captains of industry. The audience was the people of America whose need for political intrigue, scandal and self-righteous moralism would enable the most skilled actors of life to deter any ability to alter the cost of history. Then, set the stage for those chosen by the other to continue the drama – the thing that made it all super attractive was the unplanned renegade, the rogue who held no loyalty to them. The party, or the people – only the rogue was without loyalty to them. The party or the people – only the rogue could determine his destiny and become the ultimate actor by playing to those who chose him – a better than believable role of a needy control actor. E.B. Story was just such a man. Hadn't he honed his skills on the lovely Jane Graham (hyphenated) Story?

He laughed out loud. All the world was truly a stage, and all the actors played their roles flawlessly, all except for him - The rogue - He laughed again. Too easy.

Chapter Twenty-Four

On the second ring, Li Jaing Hua picked up his telephone.

"Ambassador Hua, how may I help you?" he answered as politely **and as nonchalantly** as possible. He knew who the caller was without benefit of introduction.

"Good day sir. This is the President of the United States, Stephen Story." The President needed to select his words carefully as to not degrade the recipient of his call and cause him to "lose face" in any way. Sensitive Far Eastern "feelings" could be damaged by the slightest misuse or misunderstanding of words. **His translator was well aware of the cultural differences and was very selective when converting the English to Chinese verbiage.**

"President Story. I was anticipating your call with a **complete** explanation of your country's belligerence **in** its latest military confrontation with the People's Liberation Army Navy **on Hainan Island**. We are extremely concerned in that we now have one dead pilot and the loss of a People's Republic aircraft costing millions of your dollars. The total cost of your aggression is still being calculated."

Marty Windham, the President's personal secretary, entered the Oval Office unannounced. Without speaking, he motioned for the President to release the push-to-talk button on the telephone.

"Mr. President – bad news – our downed aircraft had the new ASW **SQUALL** system on board. If that system falls into the hands of the Chinese, our submarines will be compromised. Good news – it appears the aircraft was severely damaged but landed safely on Hainan Island and the entire crew survived. The aircraft has, not as yet, been moved. Satellite coverage is poor due to cloud cover and we cannot ascertain if the aircraft has been boarded."

"Thanks Marty", the President replied while trying to collect his thoughts.

"Mr. Ambassador. The American people regret any loss of life. We are a very caring nation and the loss of any individual, Chinese or American, is regretful. I am sure than upon review of the incident involving our aircraft and yours, we will both be provided the facts of the situation and the accidental nature of the incident will be brought to light. Without meticulous review, neither one of us would want to conclude it was the others fault."

What a bunch of **bull** just came out of my mouth, the President thought. Hua knew exactly what happened above the South China Sea. The two countries have dealt with similar situations on a recurring basis throughout the cold war. Just like the Soviets and the ship bumping incidents in the Mediterranean and Black Seas as well as the Pacific Ocean; it is a game of chicken – we collide with them, the collide with us; people die; posturing from one day to the next. We apologize to them, they apologize to us and it is over – until the next incident.

"Mr. President. Skipping the rhetoric should be our first agreement. The Chinese people know the reasons for your flights over and near Hainan Island. Our signals intelligence facility on the island has been a favorite target of your electronic monitoring for years. **You are interested in our new surface-to-air missile defense capabilities.** Your aircraft was caught in the act by elements of the PLAN and while attempting to flee the area, using aggressive tactics I might add, collided and destroyed our aircraft."

"Mr. Ambassador. The American people will demand the same as the Chinese, a full accounting of the incident. We, even now, would be very foolish to assume some wrong doing. Would we not?"

"I cannot argue your point, Mr. President. I do, however, to use a saying from your western movies, have an ace in the hole. I hold the entire crew of your aircraft and they will be facing intense interrogation, make that questioning. Equally, I am in possession of your aircraft, virtually intact, with much of its equipment available for processing by our technicians. We will be able to play the tapes your aircraft and crew have provided. Your own technical capabilities and lapses in judgment will be open for the world to examine. Therefore, I believe I hold the higher ground."

Hua did not attain his current position because he was stupid, the President thought. He also knew the Chinese would exploit the possession of the P-3, its crew, and its equipment; they would also hold on to the U.S. aircraft and crew for as long as possible for the world to see. He was correct. He did hold the higher ground. **The President only feared for the fate of the crew and equally for the**

amount of information which could be gleaned from the captured equipment and data.

The President continued carefully. "Despite the loss of life, what we have here is an opportunity for solidifying and continuing Sino-American friendship. You have something or ours that we value very much – it cost us millions of dollars and its value to U.S. military and especially our submarine forces is inestimable. In fact, such a revelation should be worth several millions wouldn't you say? I think several weeks of hands-on research would be appropriate before you return our property. Oh, there will be plenty of saber rattling but no problems, Mr. Ambassador. I may have to rethink a few things – I think it time we open our relationship to public scrutiny. I suggest high level talks – soon – very soon."

Ambassador Hua would have great reward for co-opting a world leader especially the President of the United States. His legacy would be forever secure and his family would ever be able to live well. And to think all it took was a few dollars – no guns, no planes, just money. How simple it was. Soon China would not need to ask anything of anyone. They would prosper for generations. Who knows, they might even be able to annex the USA. It was good to be a player in such an exciting era. Most people, even in China, had no idea of how things really worked – neither the Americans nor the Chinese would accept that the future of their countries would be settled by non-elected officials in back room deals.

It was obvious to Hua that the President did not know the Chinese were aware of the value to the SQUALL system. During his proposed several weeks of review, the Chinese would concentrate on SQUALL and make every effort to duplicate the system and copy every code and program. **In doing so, he would cripple the command and control systems of the United States and their allies across the board.**

Things were even easier when your target was greedy and selfish/self-centered to a fault – and President Story was that. He had a history of self-indulgence back to his youth. People didn't realize how much study went into your opponent. Every important national leader, their family, advisors, friends and associates – a full life study with psychological profiles and scenarios would lend to fulfilling the co-op. Story was very easy – women, power and money – the magic trio. Plus lack of courage – always seeking the easy way – unwilling to stand for anything even his own party. Never have the American people chosen such a weak leader - nor would they again. But he would not have to worry about that. He wouldn't have to worry about anything! Did the dragon ever worry about a rabbit or a rat? The American President was in fact the result of the cross breeding of the two. The result, a sneaky, scared of its own shadow fur ball despised by everyone.

The President hung up the phone.

Ambassador Hua removed the telephone from his ear and looked surprised. He replaced the receiver on the hook.

Chapter Twenty-Five

Frank had been sitting in the pilot's seat for who knew how long. It was getting hot in the aircraft but he had no choice; the temperature started rising immediately after he shut the engines down. The Chinese had surrounded the plane with perhaps fifty soldiers armed with automatic weapons and they had, as yet, not tried to enter the aircraft nor disembark his crew. Although they had not made any moves toward the aircraft, he knew it would only be a matter of time; **they were waiting for orders and it must be just as hot standing out there in the hot sun.** The crew had continued with their emergency destruction while the plane sat on the runway.

As if they were reading his mind, a voice boomed over a loudspeaker: "Those aboard the aircraft, you will disembark the aircraft in single file with your hands behind your head. If you are armed, you will be shot without warning! You will be treated fairly as you are only pawns of your belligerent government. Any form of resistance will not be tolerated." The Chinese soldiers, with weapons ready, began moving slowly towards the P-3.

LT Christmas still had control of the internal communications. He glanced over at his co-pilot. "Mark, I don't know what to expect; I don't know what these clowns will do. We have twenty-two people to take care of and that is the bottom line". I want you to escort the crew off the plane; I will be the last to disembark".

"Understand skipper", replied LTJG Salerno as he climbed out of his seat and headed aft.

"Chief, secure from emergency destruction and get the crew ready to go. I want the crew to remember that we, every one of us, are in the United States Navy and we will act accordingly. Have Petty Officer Prescott muster the crew to ensure no one has been hurt and report back to me. I will **demand** medical attention for those that have been hurt or wounded".

"Roger that skipper. I am pretty sure everyone made it through OK with nothing more than a few bruises. That was a sweet piece of flying to get this bucket landed in on piece".

The Chinese soldiers had reached the plane and were attempting to see in to the aircraft. They were just as curious to see in, as the aircrew were looking out. The P-3 crew was responding magnificently; there was no panic, no complaints. They had methodically performed their emergency destruction and were now preparing to leave their plane in an orderly fashion. **Most of the crew had also destroyed personal items such as letters with return addresses, pictures of girlfriends and other relatives as they did not want the Chicoms to gain any information on their personalities.**

"Lieutenant, Petty Officer Prescott reports the crew mustered and no serious injuries reported. We are standing by for your orders."

Approximately five minutes had passed when LTJG Salerno requested permission to pop the forward hatch for the debarking of the crew.

"That is a go", replied Lieutenant Christmas. "Good luck to all of you. Don't give the Chicoms anything to write home about."

When Salerno popped the hatch and deployed the ladder, two Chinese soldiers immediately entered the aircraft; one with his automatic rifles leveled at the crew. In near perfect English, one instructed the crew that they would be searched for weapons before leaving the plane. Two additional soldiers stood right at the foot of the hatch with their weapons at the ready.

LTJG Salerno was the first to depart the aircraft. He was searched rather roughly but thoroughly. The Chinese soldier recognized the single silver bar on his flight suit collar and identified him as an officer and he was immediately segregated from the rest of the crew. The twenty-two remaining crew members received the same treatment as the departed single file from the plane, **each was thoroughly searched with the Chinese seemingly very concerned about weapons.** The Chinese were definitely versed in the ranks of the U.S. Navy as they **also** removed the Chief from the ranks of the other enlisted and placed him with Salerno **and Chief Warrant Officer Cutler.**

After he completed a walkthrough of the plane, LT Christmas was the last to depart the P-3. As his head exited the hatch, the apparent senior soldier asked him if he was the pilot and whether anyone else was left on the plane.

Frank replied, "Yes I am the pilot and has the PLAN forgotten military customs to have an officer of equal

or senior rank meet me to discuss the turning over of my aircraft?" (Frank had no idea if this was true but it always worked in the old cowboy and war flicks he saw in the movies and on TV. With this Far Eastern mentality of saving face, who knew what would happen here? The Hawaiian good luck sign work so he figured he would give it a shot.)

The soldier seemed stunned and unable to react. Within a few seconds, he spoke in to his hand-held radio and a commotion occurred at the bottom of the ramp. Within a few minutes, an office of the PLAN climbed the stairs of the ramp and presented himself to the arrogant young American.

The Chinese officer rendered a hand salute. "I am LT Zhang Wei Zhao, P L A N, representing my Commanding Officer, Captain Fong, at your service, Sir!" (Captain Fong would probably have him demoted for allowing this American to assume such a dominating position over a PLAN officer.

Frank snapped to attention and saluted LT Zhao crisply - "LT Frank Christmas, United States Navy. I am the senior officer aboard this aircraft and I place myself and my crew at your disposal. Please ensure my crew is treated under the terms of the Geneva Convention while under your and your government's immediate care"

"Follow me Lieutenant", replied the **Chicom Officer**."

The Chinese PLAN Lieutenant led the U.S. Naval Officer down the ramp in a strict military fashion.

As Frank passed his crew, he saluted and they, in unison, snapped to attention and returned his salute much to the chagrin of the Chinese officers and troops.

Frank's crew all tried to keep their composure as he winked his eye and flashed the thumbs up sign. Even in the most of precarious of situations, he and his crew tried their best to maintain the upper hand.

The soldier escorted Frank to an awaiting military vehicle. As the car pulled away from the aircraft, Frank noticed a troop carrying vehicle pull up to the ladder and a number of people dressed in white smocks immediately **boarding** his plane. **His crew was being loaded aboard aboard a gray bus for transport to who knows where.**

It began.

Chapter Twenty-Six

Information about the air collision and subsequent crash landing of the American aircraft on Hainan Island had not officially been released to the American public but already the rumors were being flashed on the television screens of all the major news networks. CNN had already broken into their programming with newsflash concerning the possible loss of a naval aircraft in the South China Sea – more information to follow. **It seemed like the United States could glean more intelligence from the enemy by watching CNN then they could be monitoring all the enemy communications circuits and dedicating their own intelligence gathering efforts against the enemy. Our only problem was trying to determine who, what, and when to believe who, what, and where!**

Sam and Kitty looked deeply into each other's eyes. Words were not needed in moments like this; their relationship was that deep. They both knew that Frank and his 23 crewmembers were now prisoners of the Chinese Communists and that **he** would be blamed for the entire incident. No one on this side of the world could venture a guess as to what the length of their stay would be. Sam thought back to the late 1960's when the crew of the USS

PUEBLO was held by the Communists for nearly a year **when the ship supposedly ventured** into the territorial waters of North Korea to spy on the North Koreans. **Commander Lloyd Bucher and his crew of 82 were captured in 1968.** Ironically, a single member of the Pueblo's crew died **and others were wounded** when the North Koreans fired at the ship just prior to boarding. **The remainder of the crew was tortured and beaten repeatedly at the hands of the North Koreans for nearly a year.** At his point, Sam and Kitty knew of only the death of the Chinese pilot.

Sam was additionally saddled with the knowledge of SQUALL. He knew of the peril that would visit the crew if he was not 100% successful.

They knelt and began praying for Frank – First Sam and then Kitty, praying that God would hear and provide a solution. They prayed for Frank and his crew. Sam **was not sure nor convinced that this was the type of thing that should be entered into a prayer request yet, he** prayed that when the time was right, the planted **Barnacle** virus would be **successful and its intrusion into the Chicom Command and Control networks would go undetected and be successful.** The hard part was just waiting and in reality, the United States might not find out for months, even years, down the road. **Conversely, those privy to the Barnacle virus were not really sure what the response of the Chinese government would be if such a virus was discovered. Denial of its existence!**

In reality it wasn't Frank's mission that was of a major concern – Senator Paul Webster was the real problem – a problem that was persistent – and ruthless in hunting his victims. When he was done, it wouldn't matter to him who was left in the lurch – who was broken and crushed – whose future was forever ruined. Paul Webster on the hunt; Paul Webster in the news; Paul Webster with the gavel; Paul Webster was the problem. Could Sam throw him off course? How could Sam protect that which was only being used as a shield? It could only be accomplished by a thin vale of misinformation – such a daunting responsibility.

"God", he prayed, "give me wisdom, strength and the peace that passes all understanding – for my son, his crew, and for our nation."

The alternatives were so overwhelmingly bad that . . ., he left the thought hang. He looked at Kitty again. How blessed he was to have had such a wonderful woman as his wife. She was his rudder – and together they had endured many a storm.

She knew without words what Sam was thinking. She gave him a long hug and whispered in his ear those words she always knew made Sam feel at ease.

"I love you Sam, with all my heart", she whispered and clung him to him dearly.

He sighed and let the tension flow out of him – He knew - boy did he ever. He clung to the old navy axiom "Hold Fast".

Chapter Twenty-Seven

Paul Webster grinned. He knew he would have someone dancing on the head of a pin before day's end. People trusted the Senator; his party, the other party and most importantly the people. He could easily cross party lines because the people saw him as impartial, honest and above partisan politics. Indeed he was all that, and more. He had single-handily kept the country on track, cut pork by deftly balancing needs, wants, and properly gauging press reaction to funding. Simple!

It was not only who you know in this hotbed of political iniquity, but how you used them and how you abused them. You kept an inside track on each and every one of the people in your deck. One person meant one thing on one day and that same person could be used for something entirely different on the next. That little black book, the one that is never written down but always kept up-to-date somewhere in your mind or in a computer file far from the reaches of others, under a deep, dark hidden password – every politician; a Republican, a Democrat, a Socialist, an Independent, had one and kept it to himself/herself for that inevitable day.

He quickly scanned over his team's research, specifically looking for some oversight items that he was famous for breaking during the hearings – the press thrived on his revelations as did the American public. Two terms, then off you go; here in the Senate his power remained intact. As he mused, his eye caught an expenditure of 37 million dollars from FEMA; not so unusual that, but what was the crisis necessitating 37 million dollars. He put it aside; definitely worth further investigation. He also noted a nifty 15 million dollar expenditure for Native American activities. Again, he intuitively knew this was the one to hone in on. What was it with Indians and their love for the old ways, Socialism? Hadn't they lived in squalor long enough? Squalor, squalor, SQUALL – Where was that report on the Navy? He called for his secretary and demanded the Senate Armed Services Committee's out-brief on SQUALL. Who came up with these names anyway?

Then he called his source at the Pentagon;

"Colonel, how are you? Paul Webster here"

"Hello Senator, hope all is OK up there on the hill. How may I help you?" replied the Army officer knowing full well there was a request for some sort of help to follow.

"Listen, something has come to my attention and I need some off the record support. It concerns a Navy project called SQUALL. I just need dollar figures - not anything technical', the Senator explained.

"Yes sir! That shouldn't be too difficult."

"Great, **please keep it low key, I wouldn't want to raise any eyebrows on my queries. You** have my private number. I look forward to hearing you soon; Webster replied and hung up the telephone.

It was truly amazing how things worked around Washington and the Pentagon. There was always a way to obtain information; there was always a Lieutenant Colonel wanting to make Colonel or a Colonel wanting to make General. They were the way and he was the means. He leaned back in his chair. This was Sunday and it was going to be one of his banner weeks. He could feel it in every fiber of his body. Conviction, Contacts, corroboration - The three C's of control, maybe it was the four C's.

Chapter Twenty-Eight

Jenny Soliban looked at herself in the mirror, she was pleased. Her skin was clear; her eyes were deep brown and her hair long and shiny, her body slim and athletic. Her clothing was tailored specifically to her and her attire always reflected a positive, business like demeanor. She, in fact, could be the poster child for the legal community at any locale.

It had been six years since her graduation from law school and, since the day after attaining her law degree, she was employed by Heartland Associates, the number one international law firm in the United States. Her case load was large but she was always prepared; a trait which had her climbing the ladder of success at an alarming rate. Despite her rather young age, her goal of a partnership in two to four more years was well within reach.

Jenny thought back on the major decisions she had made and realized that her time at Liberty University in Lynchburg, Virginia had set the stage for her future successes. It was a good Christian School founded by the late Jerry Falwell and his family in the early 1970's and it helped instill a strong sense of values in her and her classmates. She always professed Divine guidance in her life; from LU through to law school and then to Heartland Associates.

It was on a unrelated trip to Hong Kong that she met Frank; many thought it a chance encounter; she had a more religious mentality. While in Japan: she visited Hong Kong on a whim where she met Frank Christmas who was on liberty with the Navy. She never thought meeting Frank in terms of chance; there was a reason for everything and everything had a reason. They met on a sight-seeing tour and she was immediately infatuated with him, he **in is pure white uniform with a chest full of ribbons and, she didn't know that the called them but, two little cute gold lines on his shoulders;** they had dinner that evening and she knew that they would be together forever after. He called the next day and met every day thereafter while together in the Orient. Their relationship bridged geography when they met again in Washington, D.C. He was charming, handsome, and God-fearing; and was focused on his life's direction. There was little doubt that he would propose soon and they would live the proverbial happy every after.

The telephone rang abruptly, shattering her daydream. She didn't realize she had been caught up in her thoughts for so long.

"Hello".

"Hi sweetheart; it's Sam."

Oh, hello Sam. Good to hear from you. Is everything OK?"

"Oh, yes, everything is fine. I just wanted to give you a call to invite you down for a visit to spend some time with us in Alexandria for a week in April. It would be great if you, Kitty and I could get together for a while." said Sam smiling.

"Let me make sure I have a clear calendar – don't want any trial dates to interfere" Jenny explained. "Can you hold for a second?"

Jenny opened her calendar and, with one exception, found she would indeed by free. She picked up the telephone and said, "Looks like a winner Sam. I have one meeting that can easily be re-arranged and I can do that with no problem. Appreciate the invitation".

"Great, we can set everything up and get back you to confirm. It will be wonderful to see you". They both hung up.

Sam looked at Kitty and smiled, Jenny would be coming. Frank had asked them to arrange her visit but did not want her to know that he would be there. He had something "really important" to tell them. Kitty wondered what it could be. Sam, in his always direct manner, said that Frank wants to marry Jenny – that's what it is. Kitty sighed – if only he would settle down and marry. Jenny was a terrific and above all a Christian girl – smart, pretty and humble. She knew she could keep Frank forever.

Sam looked at Kitty and thanked God again for the wonderful woman she was. He was a lucky man and he knew it. He was never so happy as when he was with her. Too bad everyone wasn't blessed like this; there would be less strife in the world.

Chapter Twenty-Nine

Sam's phone rang, it was John. He had some inside dope on Senator Webster's current queries - FEMA was a target for a possible congressional probe. Webster's aide was bragging to his contemporaries about substantial fiduciary issues within FEMA. Most would be concerning the probable mismanagement of funds, but once they start digging it could move in to other related areas and departments.

Sam was most concerned about was this being Frank's last flight; just knowing he was safe on the ground was a beginning and an ending all rolled in to one. Sam could then rest a lot easier. Maybe he could then retire and move to some little town where the biggest event of the year was the annual 4th of July celebration complete with legal fireworks, hot dogs and apple pie. Kitty would be happy to get away from D.C. too.

He called Logan Arnold.

"Logan, we'd better talk." Sam began.

Logan Arnold was simply one of the best Chiefs of Staff any administration had had for decades. He was honest, forthright but not aggressive, and above all loyal - first to the Constitution, then to his boss. His loyalty was unquestioned and if confided in and asked to keep a confidence – he would. When Sam called Logan stopped and gave Sam his undivided attention. First, Sam rarely called. When he did, it was always, always important –

"Sam, how can I be of service?" Logan replied immediately without any questions.

"I need to speak with you privately, not on an open line, and right away!"

"Sure, Sam. When and where, you name it.

"How about right now?. I can be in your office in 20 minutes."

"Absolutely! Is it that bad, Sam?"

"Worse, Logan, this could be the one we've all worried about – but you need to keep this under your hat until we've talked – then I trust your judgment on what follows. Don't want to discuss any more over the telephone."

"OK, Sam – 20 minutes, my office. Have you eaten?"

"No."

"OK, I'll have something ready when you get here. Do I have to clear my schedule?"

"Logan, I'd say yes – and you might want to be sure no one is around"

Logan braced himself.

"Sam, do I need to alert POTUS?"

"Not just yet, Logan, but soon – I would think."

Logan knew Sam had his finger on many pulses and he wondered which pulse was pounding with the issue. He knew Sam wouldn't panic but he sounded pretty desperate. Was he aware of some larger problem with the earth quake activity out west?

"Sam, only one more question. Foreign or domestic?"

"Severe ramifications for both, very severe – even CATOSTROPHIC!

"OK, Sam, see you in 20 minutes." He hung up.

The Chief of Staff immediately rang his secretary. "Lola, clear the decks- order Chinese for two, my office 20 minutes then all of you can go home for the day." He looked in the mirror – what now? He looked towards the ceiling, "God give me strength."

Sam's knocking brought him back to focus. He moved to open the door. Lola hadn't even been able to secure the office and, of course, the Chinese food hadn't arrived as yet.

"Lola, how are you? You look great; how's the family?" Sam was always the gentleman. He always asked about things and made Lola feel comfortable even in the middle of an apparent crisis. "Is the boss in?"

"Sure Sam. He's expecting you – and I'm fine. Thanks for asking. How's Kitty?"

"She's just great. If you ever decide to change bosses, please give me a call."

"You bet I will, Sam. He's expecting you – go right in."

Sam winked as he reached for the door knob. Logan beat him to it and opened the door.

"Sam. Good to see you. Come in."

Their eyes locked full, each man realizing that this was one of those special days in history that would impact the future for decades. Sam and Logan sat in the overstuffed chairs in the corner of Logan's office by the back shelf with the large windows as backdrop. He could see the strain on Sam's face and knew that Sam would not be wasting time. The food finally arrived and the two sat, using the coffee table for the dinner.

Sam reemphasized the requirement for secrecy before he began. Before taking him back nearly a century; taking him back to that slender thread connection that now could strangle two nations and elicit a war that would forever change the America each man served and loved.

By the time Sam finished it was 11:30 PM and Logan had not even asked one question although he had many that would need immediate solutions. POTUS would, in this case, need to know his alternatives since he had no way to stop it. He wondered how he had been entwined, then realized only the Almighty Himself knew and that would have to be enough for now. These included: What day would the attempt take place?, Who would be the on-duty reactionaries for both the U.S. and Chinese governments?, and lastly, What were the Plans A & B going to be when it all went down?

Sam realized that this could be the end of his and Logan's friendship – one served the President, the other the nation. One was concerned with the political fallout, while the other was concerned only with the saving of a nation regardless the cost. One had only political concerns – the other both personal and mission outcomes.

Should they have to, each knew without speaking they would condemn the other to failure to save their cause. Both knew the end would result in a different America. How different, they would never know.

Chapter Thirty

As expected, the Chinese had segregated the officers and enlisted personnel in an obvious attempt to deter any formal chain of command from being maintained.

Lieutenant Frank Christmas, Lieutenant Junior Grade Mark Salerno, CWO4 Bob Cutler were initially separated into individual rooms but quartered in the same building. They were not however, able to communicate directly. Frank was not aware of the fate of his crew.

While unknown to Frank, his crew was settled in to what amounted to a old World War II style barracks on the other side of the PLAN base. The building was adequate but lacked the necessary environmental conditions to which Americans were accustomed. While the crew had been treated well, all personnel were wary and fearful of Chinese intentions. The American crew had reviewed the treatment of captured prisoners, particularly that endured by the USS PUEBLO crew and those captured in Viet Nam. Thoughts raced through variations; beatings, withholding of food and water, torture, public ridicule, etc. Being treated well really confused the issue among the crew. **A few of the old crew members had been through the**

old Survival, Evasion, Resistance and Escape (SERE) training and had a limited clue of what to expect. Perhaps the biggest question was why, while they waited for the other shoe to fall.

Each sailor was being questioned individually, a somewhat tedious procedure involving all 24 crew members. **Captain Fong's initial interrogation techniques could not be solidified as he did not know what techniques to use. Would it be the hardened techniques used on the captives of other Asian or Serbian countries or the soft approaches used when turnover of prisoners would be immediate. By Captain Fong's initial diagnosis was to go with the heavy application but long term prognosis called for the softer approach.**

The Chinese interrogators did not know how much time they would have until the politicians took over and their prisoners would be returned to the United States. While the questions differed with each individual, the Chinese intentionally varied their interrogation tactics in an attempt to confuse their prisoners once they were reunited with their comrades.

Chinese technicians were actually more interested in the bonanza of monitoring and intercept equipment contained in the aircraft and their technical people were swarming over the plane. Their uninhibited review of the equipment would allow them to photograph and duplicate the functions and abilities of each and then build countermeasures to protect their own future operations. Unfortunately, the American P-3 crew's destruction of technical manuals and other pertinent paperwork was nearly 90 per cent successful and provided a deterrent to Chinese efforts. The recovery of computer hard drives and programs would, however, provide all the data the Chinese needed to reverse engineering the equipment.

The Chinese guard gestured towards **Chief Petty Officer Edwards** and motioned him to proceed through the doorway on his left. As **Edwards** proceeded through the door, he was met by a scene directly out of the movies.

A table with three Chinese military members and a fourth man dressed in civilian clothes were seated behind a lengthy table. In front of the table sat a single wooden chair with a wire with a single light bulb directly above it. Right out of an old black and white move; he almost chuckled to himself at the scene.

The civilian spoke, "Have a seat. Please state your name, your rank, and your technical function on the spy plane that now sits on Chinese soil and is, by virtue of its location, Chinese property."

What a great way to begin an interrogation **Edwards** thought. He sat down on the wooden chair facing his interrogators.

"**Ralph Eric Edwards, Chief Petty Officer**", he stated. I am responsible for ensuring the officers aboard the aircraft are served coffee and are comfortable during the duration of our flight." **The Chief** figured he might as well have some fun before they started with the bamboo shoots under his finger nails. While he was scared to death, he could not let his capturers know.

Mr. **Edwards**, do not try and be a hero and impress us with your arrogance. We are already aware that you and Mr. Prescott are a Cryptologic Technicians who has **been trained to lead your crew in the intercept and processing** of both communications and non-communications signals of foreign governments, including that of the Republic of China. Please do not attempt to insult us with your attitude. You will be treated humanely throughout your "visit" on the island of Hainan. Your demeanor will define the term humanely. Do you understand?"

"Yes sir!" the Chief replied with a bit of attitude. "Ralph Eric Edwards, Chief Petty Officer, United States Navy.;"

My name is Li Qiang and I am a member of Ministry of State Security. I have been tasked with determining your aircraft's mission, its capabilities, its successes and failures. Your pilot has made my job much easier as we have your plane intact. Your technical background in operating much of the technical equipment onboard your, rather our, aircraft will, with your cooperation, make our mission much easier. Without your cooperation, we will still determine what we desire; it will just take us a bit longer. They length of your stay in our great republic will be determined by this cooperation. When you depart the room and return to your criminal friends, please relay these facts. You are dismissed **Chief Petty Officer Edwards**!"

The guards flanked JJ and escorted him back to his **barracks "room".**

As the Chinese Communists anticipated, the crew of the P3 quickly crowded around the Chief and threw questions at him as fast as he could field them. Trying to answer the questions as best as he could, the Chief conveyed the message the interrogation team had said to him.

"Be bold, but be careful", he told the remainder of the crew. "They are aware of what we do and basically what our capabilities were aboard the aircraft." I assume they are listening to everything that we are saying while we are staying in this "hotel" so, don't say what is not to be heard.

The individual interrogations continued throughout the night. Each of the remaining crew members was called before Li Qiang and each responded similarly to that of the Chief.

As expected, Li Qiang was not bothered by the response of the crew. He did not expect any of the Americans to roll over and provide him with the expert advice he needed. He would continue the "interviews" using further intimidations until one of the weaker members surfaced and then concentrate solely upon him or her. Otherwise, his own technicians would continue to concentrate on the reverse building of the aircraft equipment and its technology. His superiors would be most happy with the capture of the computer equipment and tapes the Americans called "SQUALL".

Chapter Thirty-One

As expected, LT Christmas was physically isolated from the rest of the crew and the other officers. He was their leader and, under most concepts, their inspiration. Chinese thought processes for isolating him upset the military chain of command and induced confusion among the crew. The isolation also provided time for Frank to retrace his thoughts and question his actions before, during, and after the mission. Isolation could do that to any individual regardless of their rank and training.

As he thought back, Frank knew he should not continue his relationship with Jenny. In all likelihood, **he figured** he wouldn't be alive very much longer. The slightest miscalculation; a fraction of a second's error, and he and his crew both would all be dead. **He did not know what kind of interrogation to expect and, if severe, how long he could hold out. He did not consider himself a hero, only a normal person capable of normal things.**

The burden was so heavy. Jenny was too decent a woman to be saddled with a dead-end relationship. Dead-end, how ironic - the words rang in his head. NO! He would do the honorable thing – he would call her and break it off; too many negatives. Mission failure in death; mission failure being imprisoned in China for 20-30 years, even life – how could an honorable man levy such a burden on one he loved? He prayed,

> *"O God, how can I do right with all that is before me? My nation is so vulnerable to wicked men who seek only self-fulfillment – Even our leaders are corrupt beyond redemption. The damage is so great. Almighty God, show me a way to honor you in what I must do. Amen."*

He had written Jenny a letter the day before his mission commenced. It was to be opened only in the event of his death or capture. He detailed why and placed it a safe deposit box with instructions for the key to be presented to Jenny upon confirmation of his death or long term imprisonment. Otherwise, the key would be returned to him upon mission completion. Frank hoped this arrangement would not hurt Jenny unnecessarily.

Frank wrote:

> *"My joy, words and words alone can never express what I must convey to you for by virtue of the fact you are reading this letter, our worlds have fallen apart. From the moment I first saw you, I was totally in love; overwhelmed with such a feeling that were I to never have seen you again, I would have had the greatest moment in my life. Having now loved you*

and shared all of our hopes and dreams, I know God has blessed me above all men.

The first thing I want you to know is, it's OK. Do not look to the past of what might have been, trust God for your future and seek His wisdom. I fear our nation is about to fall into its darkest hour and only God can save us from the wrath to come. I can't tell you why, but none of the mission was an accident. Every moment, every second of this mission was planned and the risks are secondary to the chances of success. Please do not dwell on anything but your survival. In a separate envelope I've given you access to my bank – the account is yours – I've notified them to surrender it to you and you are the primary beneficiary of my insurance – you deserve that and more. I suggest you divest of any stocks and securities you have and invest in land and gold. These will be of use to you should everything else go wrong. Move away from the coasts – North Central Montana is the best place I can think of – there you can go north to Canada – South back into the US and east or west in both countries. Try to keep free of banks and businesses, use cash or barter – it will become very ugly. I know this isn't what we've dreamed about but it has come to this – I expect you'll have 3-4 weeks to make your move – plan on a political falling out between the US and the rest of the world. Plan on the financial collapse of the US economy, plan on gas and electricity as either unaffordable or unavailable and plan on anarchy, rebellion and mayhem. Trust very few – believe very little and look to God. I've tried to look pragmatically at all of this – I imagine right now you are confused and hurt – next to God no one could love you more than I. As long as I live and breathe you will be the center of my every waking thought; and yet I know one day I will see you in eternity.

Take heart – it is the beginning of the new and the end of the old.

I love you. Yours to eternity

Frank

He had read and reread the letter again and again – sealed it and prepared for – he didn't know – he just knew his only direction was forward.

He decided that an explanation to his mother and father was also necessary to write a little to Sam and Kitty –

Dear Mom and Dad ...

Chapter Thirty-Two

Kitty could feel the strain in Sam – she knew that discussing it was out of the question. Sam couldn't. She decided to call Jenny; maybe planning a get together would help take her mind off of the matter. It would also give them a chance to further their bond. They would probably be spending many years together planning events for their future. Just thinking in those terms made her feel better. She picked up the telephone and dialed Jenny's number.

"Hello, Jen, it's me."

"Oh hi, Kitty."

"Jen, I was wondering if you would have some time to get together. I was thinking of planning a dinner and thought about you and wondered if you'd care to help me out? To tell the truth, I sort of need someone to talk to – and it can't be Sam."

"Sure, Kitty I'd love to. I was just thinking about you, too. What kind of dinner, a formal D.C. kind of thing or a more intimate type?"

"Oh Jenny – thank you; just a family type of dinner but I want it to be extra special. I just have this sense that I have to do this and only another woman would understand without having to explain it all."

"I know, Kitty – I know. You name it and I'll be there."

"Thanks Jen, it's going to be the first part of April. I think Frank is planning to be home on leave then and I'm sort of being selfish here but, I know he'll want to spend most of his time with you and I wanted to spend some time with you, Frank and Sam."

"OK. Kitty thanks. I'm very appreciative of how you and Sam have treated me. Anything I can do, any time, please give me a call."

"OK, Jen. How about Saturday, say around 6:30PM?"

Chapter Thirty-Three

Frank could hear movement outside his door; shuffling sounds and muffled conversations indicat**ing** multiple persons. He hadn't seen nor talked to anyone since he was escorted to this room. He knew a two armed guards were positioned at his door and he wondered why the extensive security was **afforded to him. He had made no attempt to escape.** After all, where would he go; he was a round-eye on an island occupied nearly one hundred percent by Chinese; he stood out like a sore thumb!

The isolation from his crew bothered him. **He was totally unaware of their status and his made raced with confusion;** while there were a few new guys, he had been with most of the crew through many missions; he knew their strengths and weaknesses as they did his. They placed their lives in his hands on every mission as he controlled the aircraft and, as such, controlled their destiny. **A lot of the men were experienced; there were two women in the crew also. No worries with the senior guys, Chief Edwards and Petty Officer Prescott would look after the junior men and women. He did not know what kind of threat the Chicoms would be to the women and was very concerned about the younger men in the crew. A couple**

of them were in the late teens and early twenties. Not an age to be experiencing the things they may be going through in the next few days or weeks.

Frank heard the key slide in the lock and the door opened. The two guards entered the room followed by a third individual dressed in civilian clothes. He was obviously a person of stature as the guards treated him with the utmost of respect; a sign of their Chinese hierarchy.

"Lieutenant Christmas. My name **is** Li Qiang and my position in the Ministry of State Security puts me in a position in which your welfare, and that of your crew, rests largely within my area of responsibility."

Frank interrupted the Chinese representative and asked, "Speaking of my crew, I want to know their whereabouts and status. I want, no, I demand to know, if any of my personnel have been hurt and if so, if they are receiving proper medical attention."

Qiang replied without hesitation, "Lieutenant, I appreciate your concern for your crew; your loyalty to them and theirs to you is most admirable. But, I must remind you that you are in no position to demand anything. You and your crew have violated Chinese airspace and through your belligerence caused the death of a Chinese pilot. Equally you, as a military man, have disgraced your country by providing my government with the gift of a fully intact EP-3E aircraft complete with all of your spy equipment. Your attitude should reflect the disgrace of failure and not the arrogance of a pilot who successfully completed his mission. You, sir and your crew could be shot for spying on my great nation."

"Mr. Qiang, let us not degrade our conversation with idle threats", Frank replied. "You and I both understand the implications of me landing my aircraft on your island and the fair treatment of my crew for the entire world to see. We are both aware that I did not violate your airspace: I requested permission to land my aircraft and was granted permission to do so. I have not broken any international laws and I landed a damaged plane, which was caused by your pilot, for the safety of my crew. Because of that, I am requesting your assistance in repairing my plane for the subsequent return to my own base."

"Well-spoken Lieutenant; spoken as if rehearsed many, many times. The position we are in, here and now, makes a local decision impossible. Your government and mine will bicker back and forth, confirming some things and denying others until your fate is decided. Until then, you fall under my umbrella and your immediate welfare is my responsibility."

Qiang continued. "You will be treated with the same respect that you and your crew display towards us, your capturers. We will talk with you and your crew to establish the operations of your aircraft and the equipment contained therein. Your aircraft will be stripped of its equipment with that equipment being examined in the strictest of terms. Inasmuch as we are on an unknown schedule and a restricted time frame, our technicians will be working 24 hours a day."

"With all due respect Mr. Qiang", Frank replied, "my crew, as well as I, will not divulge any information in terms of our technical operations. We are members of the United States Navy and are obligated to protect our operational procedures."

"We will see Mr. Christmas, we will see."

Chapter Thirty-Four

President Story's speech writers had provided him the final draft of the speech he was going to give the world representatives after careful and multi-layered talks. He had thoroughly convinced the Chinese that he was willing to work with them even though publicly, he would condemn them in his highly touted UN speech. After all, what authority did the UN have? The world body had not accomplished a single thing since its inception in the late 1940's. Wars raged, tyrants ruled, and people were slaughtered while all the UN did was talk. No binding solutions, just talk.

President Story and Ambassador Hua had worked out a truce: rhetoric back and forth - saber rattling but no action; decisive or indecisive. What the elected head of the United States would deliver was status quo – the cost of the U.S. doing business with China was the Chinese government continuing its repressive regime. For example, when the President spoke of Chinese restrictions on free trade costing the American taxpayer 25 billion dollars in trade imbalance, that 25 million would be the cost for the first level of technical data on the "trade" for the U.S. missile defense system.

The President figured 1 billion (that is a billion with a capital B) as his selling price. After all, a scorned man would need lots of money to buy solace. Ahhh, but he would find solace; in Sweden, in Finland, in Holland, or maybe in Costa Rica; **preferably somewhere warm that did not have extradition laws**

He started daydreaming again - he was doing that a lot lately. He wished it would all hurry up and be over. Only then would he feel free from the idiots in the press and the party hardliners. Didn't they know there is no one way – one must be eclectic, open, and free. Free – he loved the sound of the word "free". He conjured up vision after vision of his new life; bare-breasted women serving him alcoholic beverages on some tropical island. How fortunate he was. He really did consider himself the "man" - the strong man – a bigger than life, greater than great.

The shrill cry of the 1st Lady broke his trance.

"Not for long" he said under his breath - "not for long!" What was he thinking of when he married her anyway.

He had to admit, he had grown to love her at one time in his life but, the time had passed and she had now became a nuisance. He knew of her aspirations, she wanted to be what he was and he stood in her way. It was obvious to him that the only way she would succeed was if he was removed. Well, hang on sweetheart, you wish may come true sooner than you think. Trouble is the last name of "Story" may be a noose around your neck!

Chapter Thirty-Five

Now that she had the President's attention, she wanted to pitch the reason for a trip to the West Coast, in particularly Los Angeles, to engage in another of her "charity" events for the benefit of their soon coming library.

"As if I didn't have enough on my plate, what can I do for your ladyship **NOT**, the President said sarcastically.

Being used to his sarcasm and verbal abuse, Jane didn't ask about going to LA, she told him that she was going. "As you are aware she continued, the Chapter for the Advanced Education of American Children has requested me to address their members in Los Angeles. I'll combine the trip with some fund raising **efforts so that I can please the American public for using Air Force Two. I would not want to ruffle the feathers of our wonderful voters!** Just to let you know that I will be leaving shortly and will try to make you look good while I am out there."

"Excellent", replied the President. "It is always better for our married image when we are not together and you are out playing First Lady".

"Works for me too", she said immediately. "Gives me less chance to turn a corner and find you with some bimbo."

The President smiled and said, "Here we go again. Maybe some time you could act like a wife when we are alone instead of a movie critic finding some reason to be critical of my every move. **Maybe if you spent some time with me instead of chasing your own ambitions, I would not have to chase my so called bimbos.** Just go to LA and keep your image plastered on the front page of all the newspapers doing some charitable event that you could really care less about. I know the truth, the press doesn't. They believe you are sincere. I don't; you always have some sort of ulterior motive. **You, you, you and your undeniable image.**""

"Your useless opinion scores again", she said scornfully as she departed the room.

The last word is always the most important word. If he only truly knew, if he only truly knew!

Chapter Thirty-Six

Sam was committed. Regardless of the outcome, this would be the end of his involvement with both the government and the fraternity – the whole thing was too costly, not in terms of money but what it was doing to his insides. He could not bear the thought of how Kitty would react if Frank did not make it and the risk of the entire plan being uncovered. It was destroying him and he had been a "voting" member of its plan.

Sam murmured a prayer. He knew John felt the same way. The time had come to face the fact that this was not the Union they had pledged to defend. It had morphed into a valueless, communal society where gain by any means necessary was the goal. Rules had changed – survival of the fittest. No one cared who fell by the wayside – crush the careers of the non-compliant, destroy individuals, families and anything else that stood in the way. Fight the war, whoever had the most toys at the end wins!

He wondered just how long the Almighty would suffer the fools of America. He thought of how hard and long the framers labored during the forming of the Republic, whereas now politicians had breaks and junkets – political action committees had to be contended with – little of which had to do with actual governing and most to do with getting – getting rich, getting more, getting even, getting in, getting out – getting – much of the time the American people were ill served and over taxed and were so busy getting, they didn't see how badly they were being had. What a sad commentary on the once proud Republic.

He again thought of Kitty and how faithful she had been through all these years, never a waiver of support; never a regret. He knew he didn't warrant such devotion but he promised he'd work the rest of his life making it up to her – things were going so fast – could he hang on? He really had no choice he had to. Not to go down without a mighty struggle would not be like Sam at all. Regardless of the outcome he knew that everything he did was for the country. There was no self-interest, no personal cause, just duty to God and Country.

It seemed that when you cut his arm, he bled red, white, and blue. Most of his contemporaries, from the President himself, on down bled dollar signs and what can I do for ME rhetoric.

Chapter Thirty-Seven

Paul Webster grinned. He loved it when he got them. How sweet it is that he could cause another administration to have a scandal, a conviction and, most importantly, another feather for his headdress. A few more loose ends and FEMA was going down. He had to determine where all the money was going; Colby certainly wasn't keeping it for himself. He wasn't politically oriented one way or another. By all accounts he was just a dedicated civil servant. So what was he doing with all of the money?

"Blair, come in here please."

Blair entered the office and seemed to be surprised at the amount of paperwork strewn across the senator's desk. Two computer monitors were both active with what appeared to be Excel type spreadsheets. Senator Webster was always busy but he seemed totally immersed in the task at hand.

"Yes Senator?

"Blair, this FEMA thing, it just doesn't add up. Expenditures do not seem to line up with allocated tasks. Where is all of the money that FEMA spends going? It certainly isn't destined for just disaster preparations and recoveries. I've had our accountants check, recheck, and triple check and it seems as if from every disaster FEMA supported there is a rather consistent discrepancy between funding and expenditures – about 126 million short."

Blair had no time to answer when the Senator continued.

"Blair, I want you to find out what was going on in this FEMA pseudo world; outside of the disasters. I've a hunch that Brother Colby is more than he appears to be; so is FEMA. With the discrepancies we've documented, it appears we're close to finding out what."

"Not a word to anyone. We're so close, yet if we're not careful the whole thing can blow up in our faces which not only is bad for me but bad for the country. People will quickly tire of a wolf-crying Senator and with that, a wolf-crying presidential candidate has no credibility. Go about this with the utmost of discretion – the very utmost."

Chapter Thirty-Eight

Isolated, Frank's thoughts continued **to keep him occupied**; he was going over the entire mission and his related personal ordeals over and over again. Back to the beginning . . . .

Frank finished running the flight profile, checked the crew and was satisfied with everything. His aircraft was ready; he was ready. His crew had conducted many missions similar to this one; they were ready. Should the opportunity arise, they did not however, know the impact of what could come; what he would have to do with a predetermined course of action should the opportunity arise. He offered up a quick prayer to the Almighty who had seen him through every step of his life. - from the orphanage through flight school.

"Please steady me up for this one, Lord. Protect my crew from what I must do."

He thought of Jenny and the letter he'd written. Was it really the right thing to do? Well it was done now. He offered up another prayer, a prayer for good weather, unlimited visibility and calm winds – everything had to be perfect including his skill as a pilot.

He was beginning to understand that old saying - "Heavy is the head that wears the crown." He knew God would see him through; he was sure of it; just as sure as David was going up against Goliath. With a target that big how could he miss? Yet, just like David, the other 4 stones were what worried him.

First how would Jenny react, would she be able to accept it? She was a novice at military maneuvers and Washington back door policies. He knew Sam would square it with Kitty. She would understand the complications being a veteran of Washington politics. He had to keep in mind that no one outside the meeting at NSA would know the truth. It had to remain that way or the plan would not work and then all would be for naught. His responsibility for landing the plane on foreign soil would long haunt him in history. Maybe, just maybe, the truth would come out before he left this earth.

Secondly - the U.S. government; would hopefully pressure the Chinese for the crew's immediate release? He hoped he and his crew wouldn't end up like the helpless crew of the PUEBLO and remain captive for over a year. A lot could change in a year; personal feelings as well as political processes neither of which would benefit him and his people.

Lastly, how would the Chinese react? After all, they weren't exactly the paragon of justice in the world. Would they be able to hang some nefarious charge on them that would stymie the Department of State or, would they shoot first and ask questions later? They were being handed a situation that would benefit their country and supposedly set back the United States decades in military tactics and hardware.

Sitting in his small "cell", some of Frank's questions were already answered. He landed the plane successfully and now the Chinese had taken the bait. He was worried about the crew; they were innocent pawns in a chess game that they didn't even know they were playing.

Chapter Thirty-Nine

The Senate would undoubtedly open a sub-committee to look into FEMA. Sam could feel, in the pit of his stomach, the accusatory challenges by Senator Paul Webster. The man was just too good at what he did. There could be no doubt that once he started his quest, albeit warranted or not, there could be no good outcome. The phone rang – he looked at it and then braced as he picked up the receiver -

"FEMA, this is a non-secure line, Sam Colby speaking, may I help you?"

It was Kitty. She immediately explained that Jenny had called and she was very upset. She'd had received a letter from Frank and began crying immediately. Kitty had invited her over and she wanted to be sure that he would be there. With the evolutions going on, Sam was immediately put in a bad spot.

He started to apologize but Kitty wouldn't hear of it.

"Not late night tonight, Sam,' it has got to be right away. This is a crisis."

"Tell me about crisis", Sam replied. "I will be there as soon as possible but, I need to tie up a few loose ends. Give me about an hour. Are you OK?"

"I am, but I'm not. I just have a strange feeling about it and I can't rationalize it away. Jenny's a rock – she doesn't scare or crack easily and she's almost a basket case. Please, Sam, no last minute changes tonight. This is our Frank and Jenny. We have been called in – let's be there OK?" Sure he knew it was true.

"OK hon, I'll be there. Should I pick anything up on the way home?"

"Coffee, Sam? This is going to be a long night. Also, you'd better pray; I fear Frank is in over his head – way over and so does Jenny. See you in a bit."

"OK, hon see you."

Jenny couldn't believe what she had just read. She knew she was supposed to wait but she thought this was one of Frank's little pranks. What was going on? She just couldn't seem to make any sense of anything – she felt weak and found herself walking around in a stupor. She wasn't sure how long she'd been like that, but her first thought of any sensibility was to call Sam & Kitty. Maybe they might know what Frank was up to. She frantically dialed Kitty's number. It was only the third ring but if felt like an hour had passed since the first ring.

"Hello, Kitty it's Jen - Oh, Kitty," she cried and sobbed for 5 minutes before she could speak again. "Kitty, I've got to see you and Sam, it's, it's Frank. What are we going to do? Why? Why?" Kitty broke into the plea –

"Jen, sit down, take a deep breath and, from the beginning, tell me what is wrong." Jen sat on her bed and started to tell Kitty about the funny letter from Frank – how she could only think this as another one of Frank's little jokes. She quickly gave Kitty an overview of Frank's letter. When she stopped the silence on Kitty's end was smothering.

"Kitty! Kitty!?

"Yes, Jen."

"Kitty what should we do? Kitty, why?"

"Now, Jen listen. Here's what I want you to do – get a few things together and come here as soon as you can. I'll get hold of Sam and together we'll sort this out. Don't worry yet – we'll wait for you so don't worry about time. We're here for you and together will see it through, OK?"

"OK, Kitty it's – I just..."

"Jen, don't worry. We'll see it through together, OK?"

"OK, thanks, Kitty – see you in a little while."

"OK, Jen – see you."

Chapter Forty

Thinking back, Ernesto Sharp was, at first, perplexed by the questions Sam Colby asked; he could not understand the motive. Why did Sam want to know if SQUALL was susceptible to any type of computer virus? Of course it was. SQUALL was nothing more than a super computer programmed for a specific function but, it was still a computer, wasn't it? The functionality of any computer relied on the basics principals applicable to all computers. The grilling continued; Sam questioned him for hours and the answers ended exactly the same each and every time. Yes, SQUALL was susceptible to each and every virus that existed but, the computer and its associated programs was also protected by the most up-to-date anti-viruses available to the Navy

Initially, Ernesto wasn't sure why but he felt that Sam had some other motive in mind. Then out of nowhere Sam asked if SQUALL could be programmed to carry a virus so that if the system was compromised and fell into enemy hands intact, or largely intact, that it could defend itself by initiating an undetectable "counter" virus in the event of an attempted download.

Ernesto felt that there was something sinister was a possibility but he now was intrigued with what was beginning to unfold. Actually, he was pleased that Sam had probed about this and with all the effort he'd put into developing SQUALL, Ernesto now played with finding a perfect defense virus.

Initially, Ernesto thought that a simple degeneration bug rendering SQUALL useless in minutes would be good, but then he thought – the only people who would want to dissect the computer system would be one of the United States' "adversaries" - the Soviet Union, East Germany, Communist China, North Korea and/or some Middle Eastern country. He then started thinking of who the most likely candidates were: China, Russia, and/or North Korea; definitely one of those three. Add a second question, who was a developing submarine nation? Who was far from it? Who was in decline? As in all things, you are either on your way up, on the way down or you aren't in the game. Bingo! China had to be the target. How would they approach dissecting SQUALL? If China had a whole intact system or part of a system, their technology and advanced capabilities could easily be applied to advance their own systems.

"Now we're getting somewhere", he thought. "The Chinese – let me see – wonderful – the Chinese death of a thousand cuts" as he had seen in the movie; a virus that killed slowly, over time so that when or if discovered, it would be too little, too late. He grinned. This might even be more challenging than SQUALL itself. But the possibilities – the smile lessened. Ernesto had a mission- again. And it seemed Sam was going to help him out. How soon could it be done? That wasn't the real question. The real question was how devastating this could be to a potential enemy. Yes, SQUALL all of a sudden now had a true meaning. The quick, sudden storm at sea and the quick and sudden realization that over time SQUALL had killed you and you had pulled the trigger. WOW! His face hurt from the grin. That hadn't happened in quite some time. WOW!

Sam was long ago convinced that the only way the United States could slow the Chinese military advance was with SQUALL. If the Chinese thought they had a full working model of the U.S. computer system, then they would be able to track US submarines and neutralize the intercontinental ballistic missile threat or at least reduce it to a point of it becoming only nominally effective. Sam knew once they reached that level of defensive capability, the Chinese could then consider them militarily superior to the US and would start flexing their muscle in a new way.

At first, there may be seeds of cooperation with the US, but eventually it would come down to Taiwan being brought back into the fold in direct challenge to the West. Then the Sino-Soviet tandem would emerge as the dominant world power - a world power that would not hesitate to enforce their will on the rest of the world. It would only be a matter of time before this would happen and yet he hoped and prayed that SQUALL would delay it long enough that – that – that what? That the United States could clean the House and Senate of naive politicians who believed the way to peace was appeasement. That by making deals with deceitful governments some sort of Utopian go along, get along world, stability would be established. Fools! Look at the UN (world dictator HQ) – all they wanted was to weaken US stature and influence around the world – isolate and annihilate.

Sam knew this was a band aid for a gaping wound but they had to do something – and this was it. At least Logan understood. He understood so much he wouldn't tell the President. It all had to be believable and actors are all in Hollywood. The drama queens were in D.C.

God help us all.

Chapter Forty-One

Senator Paul Webster was ecstatic. After years of plying his political trade, kissing ass when he had to, and applying every legal and sometimes illegal activity in reaching his desired goal, he had finally grabbed the biggest brass ring and he had it firmly in his grasp. Simple math, just inexhaustible research and simple math had uncovered a mammoth government black operation group so deeply hidden and yet so wide open. FEMA –it was brilliant. His discovery would topple this administration and a score of his government colleagues. Repercussions would alter the course of U.S. history and our interaction with the three major players in the Far East; China, Russia & North Korea would forever be changed. Every ambassador would be recalled; every building block established over the last 50-60 years would crumble. Timing would be the critical element as always; luck was good but timing was absolutely critical.

First Senator Webster would arrange an "off the record" interview with the Deputy Director of FEMA, John Cunningham. Initial pressure would be applied "unofficially" He called Cunningham into his office.

"John, It's over, all over and sadly a few men and women who misguidedly thought they were doing a service for their country have, in truth, done it a gross disservice and for that ..."

He let John conjure up what the "for that" would be as he began to apply the misdirection. "I've asked you to chat as I'm in need of some advice. John, you know I'm not exactly a pushover when I'm onto something, and I believe, John, I am onto something – something very big indeed. But, I just can't seem to nail it completely down. That's where you come in, John. I know your reputation and credentials are impeccable, that's why I need you, a man of unquestionable integrity and discretion. I want to use you in a dual capacity."

Senator Webster loved this part – before Cunningham could pull his thoughts together, the trap will have been sprung with no way out except through the labyrinth – call it a maze with him holding the map.

"John, I know that somehow there is an illegal operation going on; I will find out who is responsible and I will bring it to an end. I've asking you for help as I want your commitment to the American people that you'll help me close this chapter in American history. With your help, John, I can keep it out of the press and ensure that those who will lose their jobs will not lose their reputations with their constituents, the taxpayers. The American people have a right; no, they have a God given right to an honest and ethical government. Would you agree, John?"

The Deputy Director replied affirmatively. John just couldn't seem to think straight or quickly enough. Where was Webster going and why with him?

"Good. I knew you would."

"John, you're with me aren't you?"

Once again, Cunningham provided a nodded agreement. His non-verbal reply was given to prolong the conversation for the sake of finding out exactly where the Senator was going.

"Good. John, I know that there is something going on in FEMA." He paused carefully watching Cunningham's face.

John felt his heart leap into his throat. He knew Webster was studying him. He screwed his face into an unbelievable contortion then threw the only curve he had.

"Yes, Senator, I know or rather I've suspected something for some time now but I just didn't want to wind up a "chicken little" and claim the sky was falling without further substantiation."

Webster was momentarily caught off guard. He expected an immediate denial. After all Cunningham was #2 at FEMA and he should have made every effort to protect his office. So, it was all Colby's game – or was it?

"John, I'll be frank with you. In two months this should all be over and, as a result of the fallout, I'll be the only electable candidate in all of Washington, DC. I will be able to ride this all the way to the White House. You deliver for me and any place you want in my administration is yours. If you double cross me..."

The Deputy Director interrupted before the threat could continue. "Senator, look, I'm more than willing to cooperate but not for a promise of a future pay off - no, sir, that is unethical. Why you yourself just stated moments ago that "the people have a God given right to ethical government"... and they do, Senator, that is why talk of some future position in your administration would be...well, unethical. Wouldn't you say?"

Paul Webster sat dumbfounded. Twice this second echelon bureaucrat had knocked him off his perch. He needed to regroup a minute.

"Of course, John of course you're right. I, ahh, I just want to get to the bottom of this; the sooner the better. Now it seems to me what is obvious. You are an upright and honest man. A reliable sort who when push comes to shove, does the right thing regardless of where the chips may fall – am I right?

John had been studying Webster's every word and facial expression and decided he was like most of DC, a self-centered megalomaniac determined to become President. His intent was the destruction of others to realize his own selfish ambitions. Why was DC so full of these types? A better opportunity would be to maybe have a fishing accident. Say, 50-60 miles out to sea.

"Yes, Senator, and for that reason alone I do not feel comfortable talking about it here."

"Go on, John – where? "When?"

"Let's say Saturday, we go fishing. We can take my boat out, just you and me and a tape recorder. I'll give you everything I know plus the paper work to support most of it – and, Senator – please don't talk this up. I'll have to live through it to the end. Any leaks and the end may be sooner than I'd like. You understand, Senator, this is the end of my government career; quite possibly my whole way of living. I just can't go about it here and now."

"Of course John, there is a lot of merit in what you say. Here's what we'll do - I have some clearing up to do with my schedule to free up Saturday, I'll have to – no, I don't have to explain. I'm just going to take off. Thanks, John. This may turn out to be the best thing that could happen. What time Saturday and where?"

"Well, Senator, how about we meet at Callie's at the PAX River marina – 5 AM – Saturday. I'll drive to the marina and we can get away before anyone in Maryland knows you're there."

"Right, John. Say, could we actually do some fishing. I'd like to bring something back."

"Sure Senator Webster – sure. See you at 5 then?"

"OK 5 AM on Saturday. You won't regret this, John – mark my words."

Chapter Forty-Two

Ambassador Hua fumed at his totally unsuspected recall. He could not understand why his party had disgraced him after all the hard work and compromise he had performed. A disgrace; he was now a disgrace to his family, his friends, and himself. Why? What madness. Hadn't he cultivated the sitting U.S. President and fully compromised him? Hadn't he neutralized the U.S. military through their own President? Hadn't he elevated China to a world-wide status where the country was destined to be the most powerful nation on earth? He, and he alone, had planted the seeds for China's future to rule the world.

As the arbiter and settler of all disputes, he would not stand for it. What dog had sneaked up behind him and sank their fangs deep in his back? What snake had managed to slither its way into his house and strike him? He would find out – he would. He would exact revenge and banish the traitor and his family to the farthest place on the planet; the sorriest place where they would stay until their children's children were old. No matter what the cost – whoever he had to break, he would find out and exact his revenge. He would need to be subtle. Rage would not be the way to find out. Gifts, platitudes and Kowtow – he, in the end, would prevail. But wait – what if it was a conspiracy? Who would be the best served by such a move?

"Hua", he thought, "you are far too clever for whomever it is that has unleashed this betrayal. Be it one or fifty-one, he would find out, he would be sure he'd had them all. Yes, revenge is a dish best served cold. Whoever stated that knew something about it."

He first needed to list possible suspects who would gain the most from such a move. Who would be influential enough to persuade the Party leaders to vote him out? Who would have that kind of case against him? Who would be close enough to him to be able to construct his downfall without him knowing? The even bigger question was why? He had been careful not to offend anyone, not to make enemies and not to...not to – wait – that was it. It wasn't anyone, it was himself. He had not been ruthless enough. He had not crushed enough onlookers to draw the right kind of attention to himself. But that will change. This was a test. He must be under consideration for a promotion – of course it wasn't a recall for failure. Now he needed to rethink the whole thing. What would they possibly have for him that they would recall him from a position that he so far exceeded in ways no one even dreamed of? Recall – Recall – it as his lucky day. A time to sing; his honor would be magnified a hundred fold.

Chapter Forty-Three

Jenny was determined that she would, with God's help, survive this test of uncertainty and that she and Frank would put this episode behind them and move on. She knew of Frank's devout religious convictions, that he was a professing Christian not ashamed of this belief in God; of his loyalty and devotion to service and country and his love for his parents. All of these qualities made him just the man for her. All she could do now was pray and spend as much time with Sam and Kitty as possible. The vigil she vowed would be her way of joining Frank in whatever it was that he was doing. All that mattered was that she too would pay a price. This would be a time when their love was tested and would emerge even stronger than ever – a love of a lifetime.

It struck her just then that she too would write a letter to Frank, sort of a response to his letter. Then as the years passed they could reread the letters and be even reminded of how there are no guarantees in life except that one day it will be done and each will meet his maker and begin a life that is beyond anyone's wildest dreams.

She began to write:

"My Beloved Frank:

I know the only way you will ever read this letter is if you somehow come back to me and for that I praise God forever. Although I don't know what it is that you're doing exactly, I know that somehow it is almost bigger than life. I also know that it must be so very serious and compelling that it took all you had and left me with a paper good-bye. Yet, a good-bye that was also a commitment that anyone could see was for eternity.

So my darling, until you come back to me...and you will! I'll spend my days and nights beseeching God, interceding on your behalf for a safe return for you and your crew. Also know this, Mr. Christmas, Lieutenant Frank Christmas – once you get back here, I'm never going to leave your side again. I want to be with you every second of every day as long as we both shall live, Amen! So be careful, be prayerful and know this - God's will be done. So come home, Frank – soon. I love you and I'm waiting for as long as it

> **takes. So stead up, LT., level off and bring
> that ship home. That's an order!"**

> **Love Jen.**

She felt better. Now she had one more very important thing to do. She prayed.

"Dear God, We don't know where he is or why he's there, but You do. You know Frank and his crew; provide for them and keep them in the hollow of you hand. Bring them all home safe and may your name be glorified in all the earth."

Chapter Forty-Four

When the American P-3 made its emergency landing in Hainan, Commander Dong was ecstatic. What a coup! An American spy aircraft, complete with equipment and crew was available for display in China and to the world. Moreover, the equipment was available for China's technicians to examine in detail and, if stumped, have the American crew available for an explanation on exactly how the equipment worked.

`Thinking back to the capture of the USS PUEBLO in the late 1960's by their North Korean allies, China could parade the spies in front of the world as proof of the United States' violation of Chinese sovereignty. His country could not however, make the same mistakes of his North Korean brothers. China must not allow the trickery of the American captives to exploit the generosity of their capturers by turning the propaganda photographs against them. Who could ever forget the photograph of the PUEBLO crew in which they had secretly extended their middle fingers in defiance of the North Korea; a kind gesture turned into a propaganda victory for the American crew. In the long run however, the Americans paid the price.

Today, the Executive Officer loved everyone, even that dog Captain Fong. Yes, today all of their fates changed – a promotion – a transfer and no more Captain Fong. Yesterday – yesterday – HA – today – today was the day. He had prepared the staff well. They would be very strict with the Americans, but not cruel. The world would be watching Hainan and there would be no messing up – officers and enlisted separate quarters; interrogations, but only as a formality. They had dumped the very gate to heaven in his lap. Who could have known – what the party leaders wanted, they now have - a 100% tactical military advantage over the U.S. He could feel himself giggling inside. "So lucky – so very lucky", he thought; "but where to request reassignment? Where, where, where? Really need to sit down and . . .

The phone rang.

He remembered the conversation clearly.

"Commander Dong."

"Dong, you idiot, this is Captain Fong. Where have you been? I have been trying for the last hour to find you. How come you are not here in operations? Don't you realize what is going on? How did I wind up with an idiot like you for an executive officer? I should send you to Chengdu as laundry officer. Get to my office at once and bring everything you have on U.S. P-3 Orion aircraft and its intelligence systems – if you feel you can spare me the time."

He slammed the phone down and Dong let out his best ever stream of insults. He even cursed the dust mites in Fong's quarters. How could such a crude and loathsome being reach the rank of Captain? The rank of Captain, yes, he would soon become Captain Dong. It was a shame that his forthcoming promotion would not knock out his derelict Commanding Officer; Fong needed to be exiled to some far away land that did not have a Navy. Fong would probably move up to Fushan and he? He would move to the Shanyang as Commanding Officer. Small and yet full of possibilities.

Fong – Fong - Fong, rhymed with Kong – Kong – Kong. What a disgrace to the gorilla.

Heya! Time to go.

Chapter Forty-Five

Frank was proud of the crew. A few days had passed since he had landed the plane on Hainan Island and things had actually gone much better than he had anticipated. Although separated from the crew and unable to communicate directly, word got back to him concerning their fair treatment and conditions. They had not budged an inch; they performed as he knew they would and now, as "guests" of the People's Republic, he knew they could endure for a while. He did not know however, how long the Chinese would remain patient or the determination of his own government in seeking their release.

Frank thought back over the last few days.

After sitting on the aircraft for over an hour, the Chinese finally made their initial move by instructing the pilot and his crew to exit the aircraft through the forward most hatch. His crew was understandingly worried; seeing about fifty armed soldiers surrounding the plane would cause anyone and everyone to be a little apprehensive. No one knew exactly what they faced as the filed off the aircraft with their hands raised in the air. Frank had ordered his fellow crew members to leave their firearms, with clips removed, on the plane.

The Chinese appeared very organized but the presence of their weapons put the American crew in an obvious bad light. The crew was directed to couple their hands behind their heads and sit in rows about twenty five yards from the plane. The crew dragged their feet on everything, even the simplest order, pretending to not understand the broken English of the Chinese soldiers which caused confusion by both the captives and the capturers. It seemingly incensed the Chinese officers who took out their anger on their own troops. Once seated, four Chinese soldiers commenced a search of each individual crewmember, treating their captives roughly but carefully.

The Chinese had immediately segregated the officers and enlisted crew in an obvious effort to disallow or break done any attempt to continue their chain of command. The Chinese officers seemed thoroughly familiar with U.S. Navy ranks and insignia as they immediately began dividing the crew by rank. The ranking Chinese officer removed Frank, his copilot Mark Salerno, and the cryptologic officer, Chief Warrant Officer (CWO) 4 Cutler, from the remainder of the crew and extracted them from the immediate area. Whether by oversight or ignorance, the Chinese let the Chief remain with the remainder of the crew. Under armed guard, the American officers were loaded into a troop truck and whisked from the scene. The rest of the crew remained on the tarmac.

Most of the crew had removed and discarded their nametags from the front of their flight suits and their rank insignia from their collars making their identification a bit more difficult for their capturers. As such, the Chinese held a "paper muster", directing each American to provide their name and rank to a Chinese stenographer who physically wrote down the information. During the muster, the crew watched Chinese technicians board their aircraft and remove just about everything removable. Some of the equipment and remaining paperwork was loaded into enclosed vans for transport to who knows where.

Funny how it all went as perceived. Frank wondered if the President would ever realize what a price he'd extracted in order to feather his own nest. He doubted it.

So far the Chinese had been less antagonistic than he'd thought they would be but they weren't out of the woods yet. They were alive with no serious injuries and, under the circumstances, being treated fairly. He figured since they weren't brutally aggressive right away things must be hot politically. The Chinese would, of course, denounce them as spies and threaten them; but they had SQUALL. At least they thought they did. Time would tell, but he felt as though it went very well. The timing of the hit on the F-8 was nearly perfect. He'd hoped the pilot got out okay but, realistically, he knew the pilot had ridden his aircraft into the sea. After they landed and he saw the damage to the P-3 he was actually amazed they landed in one piece.

Frank thought back to Jen. He hoped she hadn't read his letter but he knew better. What a mistake he had made. It one was thing to be able to explain quickly and another to be isolated as a prisoner of the Chinese Communists and unable to communicate. He thought how she would be reacting.

As was expected, Frank and the other two officers were housed, albeit separately, in the same building. Communication between them was all but impossible.

Dependent upon the length of the stay, they might be able to invent a means of communications similar to that used by the prisoners at the infamous Hanoi Hilton during Vietnam. Time would tell. They were provided clean, bright orange, single piece overalls and were stripped of all rank insignia.

Interrogations were daily with most emphasis placed on the exact location of the aircraft and its mission. Any obvious incursion into Chinese airspace could not be admitted and they must remain committed to the mission statement of conducting air operations and weather research over international waters.

The remainder of the crew were afforded similar "uniforms" but were isolated in three separate and distinct buildings all of which were windowless with no possible access to the outside world. The three female crewmembers were segregated in another building. There were no clocks and only limited lighting; probably an attempt by the Chinese in "time deprivation".

Interrogation of the enlisted personnel was conducted twice daily with each segment lasting about 4 hours. Questions were much quicker and the Chinese expected exact answers. The enlisted questioning was much more direct and centered on the operation of equipment, communications, and most importantly, SQUALL. The Chinese held the upper hand; they were in possession of all the equipment and portions of the unclassified operating manuals.

The Chinese did not seem too concerned with LT Christmas or LTJG Salerno. CWO4 Cutler and the enlisted personnel were better targets; they knew how to operate the computer and intercept equipment and that generated the most interest.

Frank's faith in God never altered and his concern for the welfare of his crew was paramount. Once more he fell to his knees as it was time for an evaluation of life and to thank the Lord for the providential care of his crew. Ending his prayer with a fervent AMEN, he wondered what would be next.

Chapter Forty-Six

The water was calm with just the two of them in the boat. They hadn't said a word during the short boat ride for their "fishing trip." Paul Webster sat dumbfounded. The entire evolution had just taken on an altogether different twist. FEMA was nothing compared to what would the unfolding of his last hurrah.

One he had it clear in his mind what the President had done, then he made the deal with Cunningham. It was absurd to think President Story could out maneuver this; the audacity of the man. Webster knew he would have to be extremely careful on how he continued from here; one slip up and he could well become the prey instead of the hunter.

It was clear that Colby and Cunningham had no political ambitions at all. They were the exception to the rule in the DC arena; they would never divulge anything. In fact, Webster believed they wouldn't stand in his way if he wanted to broker the end of the current POTUS. He also knew that this would be the ultimate triumph, the catapult of all catapults. The problem was the press. They did not seem to wish to see Story fail despite all his transgressions. He was positive, in fact, that they would turn on anyone internal to the Washington scene who directly challenged the President.

External influence remained however, an enigma. Who could undermine the American President and sustain such a position for the longer term? Obviously not an ally or an adversary, it had to be a neutral country, neutral to both the United States and China. The field was not wide open: India – no; Pakistan – no; South Korea – no; Japan – no. Broaden your horizon, it did not have be a Far Eastern nation; the Middle East could suffice. Egypt - no; Israel – obviously not; Libya – equally obvious; Turkey? Turkey, the country had unknowingly set themselves as the perfect player as a certain unnamed Turkish diplomat had recently revealed to the Secretary General of the United Nations that there was rumor of a high level U.S. politician supplying restricted U.S. military data to an undisclosed foreign power.

Once started, the rumor had taken own a life of its own and someone clandestinely throwing gasoline on the fire would certainly create a festering problem. Webster could publicly vow to follow the trail, wherever it led, and bring to justice those involved. He would, of course, start with a red herring – someone in the Department of Defense – he would consult with the President who would obviously throw anyone and everyone under the bus to save himself. The finger pointing would turn to accusations and the FBI, DIA, CIA all would struggle to find out but not reveal. But the secret service would let it slip out. He would have to inform the American people and then see to it that impeachment proceedings would begin. Sadly, if the President would agree to step down he could broker a deal and shut it all down; tragic, but necessary. All of this flashed through his mind in a second.

"Cunningham, you're absolutely sure of this?"

"Yes Senator, absolutely!"

"What about this plane in Hainan?"

"What about it, sir?"

"Will it cause us any problems? I mean, will it present a diplomatic hot potato for the President, what with him on the payroll?"

"No sir. I believe the Chinese are very wise. They will milk it for a little red facing but they won't tip the apple cart over. After all they own the cart and the apples."

"Yes, yes of course, and to think I was going after the good guys. Well, Cunningham back to the pier. I have to get back to D.C. pronto. If I need to contact you I'll send a message about fishing again. Call me at this number. It is my private cell number. I don't expect you'll actually be hearing from me, but just in case. Thanks, Cunningham, very few men would have trusted me. I won't forget it."

"Neither will I, Senator, neither will I."

John was glad he'd taken the risk. If Webster hadn't reacted as he did. Well, he was thankful he didn't have to go there – thankful Frank's mission was successful and thankful that the end of this saga was near at hand. It would be good to go home tonight. Maybe he'd start to think about retiring. If he was a cat he'd used up 8 of his lives and he wanted the 9th to be... what a stupid thought. He had to help get Frank and the crew back.

They did not catch anything.

Chapter Forty-Seven

The First Lady finished the last of her drink and said good-bye to the last of her well-wishers. The ride back to the hotel seemed to take an eternity. It was nearly three AM when she opened her door to the Presidential sweet, kicked off her shoes, and poured herself a final night cap. The trip had been well worth making and her support from the Golden State was nothing short of phenomenal.

She walked into the bathroom and turned the shower on, took off her clothes and slipped into a robe. Her flight was scheduled for two PM she made a mental note to schedule a return trip soon.

Walking to the sofa she felt a little unsteady, had she too much to drink? She didn't think so as she was very much in control of her alcoholic consumption. Wait, she felt it again! Then, she heard a loud cracking sound.

She stood and walked to the window to look outside when it hit -the earth quake shook the building like a dog shakes a rag toy in its mouth.

She watched in horrified slow motion as the Los Angeles skyline disappeared from her view as the buildings collapsed almost like dominoes in the window of her the Presidential Suite. The floor caved in while the large window simultaneously shattered, in front of her shattered, imploding sending large shards of glass into the room. She didn't feel the foot long razor sharp piece that imbedded itself in her neck, she looked down and saw her robe covered in blood and her thoughts only were of concern of getting the stain out of the robes.

The floor beneath her disappeared and she felt herself plummeting down **from the top floor of the hotel. She would never know about reaching the bottom as she was dead before her own hotel would become another domino in the Los Angeles skyline. The entire city would be reduced to rubble in minutes and casualties would be massive.**

Chapter Forty-Eight

It was 7 AM Eastern Standard Time. The White House internal telephone positioned next to the President's bed rang loudly. On the second ring, the President rolled over sleepily and picked up the receiver. It will be very satisfying to retire and not face the gray clouds which always seem to hang over his job. It seems he could never a peaceful moment. He did not expect good news. At least the motor mouth was not lying next to him.

"Mr. President. It's Marty, sir. I have bad news Mr. President, terrible news."

"Yes, Marty? What?" the President asked while trying to shake the cobwebs of a deep sleep.

"It's….. most of California, sir. It's – it's gone."

"What do you mean it's gone, Marty? Give me a second here; start at the beginning!" The President rose from bed and put on his robe.

"10 minutes ago, sir. A 9.5 earthquake struck California and resonated from Fresno down to San Diego. Reports are coming in of a second 8.9 quake off of the Redondo Beach area – the place is destroyed, sir."

Story came instantly awake. The President may be an SOB in political scheming but he was quick to respond to any emergency affecting the welfare and citizens of the United States. "Marty, what are the casualty estimates?"

Marty replied immediately. "First estimates are 1-1.5 million dead and another 4.5 million missing or injured. Travis AFB is gone! LAX is gone – it is just totally gone, sir."

"OK, Marty, I need you to calm down and gather yourself. G**et the Chief of Staff over here as soon as possible; I want Sam Colby and the Joint Chiefs of Staff at the White House emergency meeting room immediately; let them know to get in touch with National Guard commanders from Nevada, Utah, Oregon, Washington and Idaho for the full mobilization of all units. Get the Red Cross mobilized at whatever levels necessary to provide local assistance. What have emergency responders indicated?"

"Sir, there has been little emergency response as nearly all units have been destroyed. Sam Colby is **already** on his way to Nevada to set up a command center to direct the entire situation. Communications to the stricken area are non-existent. We are operating completely in the blind."

"Marty, I will be in the situation room within a few minutes. I will need to address the American people as soon as possible. I want as much information as we have to broadcast to them; they need to know the truth as soon as possible. I do not want the news services to broadcast any misinformation; I want everything verified before release.'"

"The military indicates the entire city of San Diego is unserviceable; the Navy has mobilized what little they have left and are being held at bay by the destruction and debris. They don't think they can do just about anything for about 24 hours. All serviceable Navy ships have departed the San Diego Naval Base in preparation for follow-on tsunamis;

they had trouble clearing the harbor due to the debris. By then the toll will be catastrophic. The press is waiting. I will have a statement for your review immediately. We can be on all the networks in 3 minutes."

"Sir. We have no word on the First Lady. She completed her fund raising event late last night LA time and returned to her hotel. There has been no communications from her or her Secret Service team."

The President had not thought of his wife. He was sure that any and all efforts to ensure her safety were well underway. He is job took priority; his wife's situation would have to wait; her survival was no different that the survival of any citizen.

"One additional thing Mister President", Marty said. "Chinese Ambassador Hua was at LAX on a layover, waiting for his flight to DC. There is no indication that he survived; I am afraid he's gone too, sir".

The President replied, "Is there anybody of importance who wasn't in LA?"

The television was tuned to CNN as usual and the first pictures of LA were appearing on the screen. They President paused briefly to observe the carnage. As much as he despised his wife, he knew she was somewhere in the middle of that mess and he mentally told her to take care of herself until he could sort out what was happening and then direct rescue personnel to her location.

The situation room was already a buzz when the President walked in. Everybody immediately stopped what they were doing and stood to show their respect.

As he entered, the President said, "Please don't stop what you are doing. We don't have time for all the etiquette bull."

TVs in the situation were turned to every major news service in the country and the scenes were gruesome. Bodies were everywhere and the skyline of Los Angeles was totally unrecognizable; it looked lie pictures of Hiroshima and Nagasaki in August of 1945! Fires burned everywhere, people were wandering aimlessly' scenes of small children wounded and crying were the most heart wrenching. The President shook his head. "We need to get help to these people immediately", he said loudly.

Marty handed the President the proposed statement to be read to the people of the United States. He read it quickly.

"Thanks Marty. Looks good; I will probably deviate here and there as I see fit. Are all the players on their way?"

"Yes sir! I took the liberty of inviting the Vice President", replied Marty just as Logan Arnold entered the room.

"Logan, I am going on the air in 2 minutes. Scan the statement Marty provided and make any necessary corrections. Ambassador Hua was apparently killed at LAX. We will have to deal with that and the P3 crew later. Jane is also in LA; I have no information regarding her status."

The cameras and audio equipment was ready to go. The meeting room filled quickly and included representatives from all the major news networks and newspapers from across the country.

The President stood behind the podium and looked into the eye of the center camera. The technician completed his countdown and signaled the President to begin.

"My fellow Americans, it is with the gravest heart that I inform you that at 3:49 AM Eastern Standard Time, two devastating earthquakes struck California splitting the state in two all along the San Andreas fault. The first quake centered 3 miles outside of San Francisco measured a 9.5 on the Richter scale. The second, an 8.9 quake, centered 2 miles off of the Redondo Beach area. **Underwater landslides caused by the earthquakes have triggered t**sunamis **may they may be** expected at any moment and the loss of property and life is catastrophic.

We are coordinating with all agencies and will have an update within the hour. There are presently limited or no communications in to or out of southern California. The restoration of communications is paramount to coordinate rescue efforts. The entire U.S. government has been mobilized and all efforts to keep the remainder of the country informed of rescue efforts are of the highest priority. It is now 4:32 AM and I will be departing for the west coast as soon as possible. All Americans are encouraged to pray to the Almighty for our fellow countrymen who live or are visiting the stricken areas. This will forever alter the future of our country.

I promise each and every American that I will mobilize our entire country to provide aid to all those citizens effected by this natural disaster and I will ensure that all information available to me is promulgated as soon as possible to keep you all informed. Thank you and God Bless America."

The President could not help but notice one the camera monitors displaying his wife in the middle of her possible last fund raising effort which took place the night before. She would be happy that her image was still being presented to the American people, despite all that was happening around her. Incredible, he thought to himself.

The reporters in the briefing room immediately stood and began shouting questions to the President but he departed the room without another word. Further briefings would be provided for transmission from on Air Force One. The President was being hustled out of the building with Andrews Air Force Base his immediate destination. His helicopter was already being prepared for his departure.

As the President was ushered through the halls of the White House, his only thought was "God Help Us All!"

President Story headed out to his helicopter and was immediately hustled aboard without any comment. The helicopter rose immediately and turned TOWARD Andrews Air Force Base.

As the President settled in to his seat, he was informed that an estimated 100 foot tsunami had all but leveled the San Francisco Bay area, literally wiping San Francisco off the map. Casualties continued to mount with no end in sight. The major portions of some of the most populous areas of the United States had been obliterated by Mother Nature. About the only thing remaining of the Bay Area were skeletal pieces of buildings and dead bodies strewn everywhere.

The President peered out of the window. "Now what?" he asked no one in particular.

Chapter Forty-Nine

It would take a little over three hours for Air Force One to navigate across the United States for a landing in southern Nevada at Nellis Air Force Base. Nellis was picked because it got the President as close to the catastrophe as possible. While a four and a half hour drive, the distant could be covered much faster by helicopter.

During his flight to Nevada, the President was being updated as quickly as possible on the status and response to the earthquake. It had been confirmed that his wife was staying at the Four Seasons Hotel in Beverly Hills and the hotel was in ruins. Without the availability of communications, her status could not be confirmed. President Story was a realist and the fate of his wife seemed sealed.

Although pictures remained unavailable, the President knew that the Los Angeles skyline had been altered forever. Tall buildings were not the norm in LA due to the recurring quakes. The U.S. Bank Tower highlighted most pictures of LA in that the building was 73 stories high and stood out in any picture. He had already been informed that the tower was in ruins

With the earthquake occurring during the early morning hours, most people would have been home and in bed. He hoped that this would factor in and reduce casualties. The freeways would have been relatively empty. Those up and about would be partiers or night workers trying their best to allow the city to keep functioning.

"Mr. President, we are beginning to get sporadic communications established; some pictures by the news agencies are becoming available. They are pretty gruesome", stated the Air Force Colonel.

"Any word on Mrs. Story?", the President asked.

"No sir, not as yet."

The President made his way to the briefing room. Upon entering the briefing room, the President was immediately bombarded with four televisions had been set up to monitor ABC, NBC, CBS and CNN. Each TV provided the same bleak picture; LA was virtually gone, San Francisco was almost completely under water and San Diego was devastated. Infrastructure which had connected the cities was non-existent; main arteries were either destroyed or underwater. They were all unpassable.

People in the briefing room were sobbing; nearly everyone was seeking divine guidance in some sort of way. Of course, when the President walked into the room, all eyes were upon him. After God, he was the person that all aboard the plane and others across the United States would be turning to for strength. All of his inadequacies as President were forgotten. He was the leader of the country; now he must lead.

Chapter Fifty

The entire world reacted in many different ways. It seemed very unusual this time. Instead of the United States providing the initial response in providing financial and humanitarian aid, other countries were quick to respond. Despite the negativism and propaganda levied at the Western world and in particular the United States, disaster always negated politics and prompted the good in people to rise to the top. In most cases, that was happening now.

Air Force One was swamped with pledges from nearly every major country on earth. The aircraft, currently enroute to Nellis Air Force Base in Nevada, was serving as the command and control center for the President and all communications concerning the catastrophic event were being routed through their command center for coordination.

The President intended to declare martial law with a dusk to dawn curfew in the affected areas but due to the expanded geographical area, law enforcement and the military would have a difficult time enforcing such a move. Unfortunately, this type of catastrophe brought out the bad in people as well as the good. In today's world society, the almighty dollar would rise above sympathies and some would be out to take advantage of those suffering. Price gouging and hoarding of necessities such as food and water would be major areas of concern.

Foreign nations were lining up with pledges of aid – financial, rescue equipment and first responders, food, medicine, and clothing. Countries from England around the world to Japan and Australia; the communist countries of Europe, Middle East countries like Saudi Arabia and even those in Africa as well as the Far East pledged whatever help required.

Some, specifically one, had both good intentions and ulterior motives. China was one of the first to respond. They were already aware of the loss of their ambassador in Los Angeles yet, they pledged their support in every endeavor. Equally, they were also the first to sense the end of the United States. Financially, they sensed the end of the U.S. as a world power; the loss was insurmountable and even the strongest nation on earth could not sustain such an impact; it would cripple them. A natural disaster would accomplish that which the Chinese government and military could not; a splinter would be removed and the way would be cleared for China to pursue some immediate goals. China would secure the Spratly Islands as well as the renegade Taiwan and it would be quick and final. The communist government would demand the U.S. pay its debts which would bankrupt their economy. The U.S. would soon be out of the way – it would be good – leave them stuck between the feckless Canadians to the north and the dysfunctional Mexicans and South Americans in the south. They would squabble for decades and remain ineffectual in the world wide stage.

It was a great day for China! Let the Americans in Hainan go – a token of our generous support for our American friends. The incident of 24 American sailors captured by Chinese forces was of little significance now. We'll let the Americans fly their own plane back to Okinawa and even recognize their heroic abilities. They were in the process of completing their examination of the American aircraft and the documentation of operational activity of the equipment onboard. Most important of all, they had the complete set of software involving the SQUALL system, the most advanced submarine and missile defense system in existence. They would soon be able to duplicate the system and upgrade their own command and control to use the system against its inventors.

Today, China, at last, will be the world's lone super power and we will not be shy in using this status to our full advantage. Who could stop us? Russia would be busy re-subordinating its rogue republics; the pitiful Europeans have no will – the world is ours and the future is bright. Call all ambassadors home. We will reorganize the world next week. America is no longer any threat to us. We can now fulfill our manifest destiny. We have been plundered for centuries and now the fullness of our time is come and we will be ruthless in exacting retribution from the English, the Japanese and the South Koreans. Next we will secure our borders with Russia and then the Won will become the world's currency. China would be the world's "Tai-pan". It was good to be alive, it was good to live now. It was a blessing to be Chinese - Heya!"

Chapter Fifty-One

The skylines of Los Angeles, San Francisco, and San Diego as well as all of the smaller cities in between were no longer recognizable; the earthquake and follow-on tsunamis had altered the lives and livelihoods of millions of southern Californians. Complicating matters was total loss of communications which hindered the ability of first responders to coordinate rescue efforts.

The first pictures of the disaster were being provided by local news media and centered on video from helicopters stationed on the outskirts of the devastated cities and flying over the area. Los Angeles and San Diego appeared as a series of major fires burning through anything that burn; most buildings were nothing more than piles of rumble – few remained standing. San Francisco was largely underwater; there was little human movement in any of the pictures or video.

Air Force One continued its flight to Nevada and what little news that was available was being monitored closely. The President remained in the private quarters of the aircraft while his staff and communications personnel were in contact with supporting elements on the ground. Television monitors located throughout the aircraft were tuned to local affiliates on the ground which, in turn, used input from every major network. As part of their coverage news stations were pleading with the rest of the American people to limit telephone calls to the affected areas. They explained that cell phone relay towers had been eliminated in southern California and that making contact was virtually impossible. What communications that were available needed to be used for the coordination of rescue operations. The remainder of the United States was in a panic. Friends and relatives of those living in southern California were making every attempt to communicate further tying up coordination efforts.

President Story had declared martial law throughout what was left of California to ensure that some resemblance of law and order was provided. The orders had gone out almost immediately following the catastrophe but he had to depend on the abilities of his military to ensure that such order would be provided. He knew the capabilities of both the active duty military and the National Guard; he was sure that once activated, the military would be setting up communications centers and providing the equipment for communications relays. Sitting on his aircraft without any ability to communicate was without precedence. At least he had communications with the remainder of the United States.

"President Story", started his Chief of Staff. "I am very sorry to have to inform you that the hotel in which your wife was staying was totally destroyed with no one being evacuated. The entire building has been leveled. We are assuming that Mrs. Story and her entire Secret Service detail have been lost."

President Story stared at Logan Arnold without replying. "Mr. President?" he repeated. "I am sorry."

"I heard you Logan and thank you for informing me. If you don't mind, I would like a few minutes alone."

"Yes sir."

The President sat down behind his desk and immediately looked at the picture of him and Jane during a much happier time. While his relationship with Jane Story had slowly deteriorated over the years, he still loved the woman despite her inadequacies and her quest for power. He had not been the ideal husband and for a brief moment, he regretted his skirt chasing episodes and wished he had been more dedicated to his wife. Too late now.

President Story knew he had no time for personal feelings. Despite the current catastrophe, he was still the leader of the most powerful country on earth and he needed to lead it without fail.

President Story realized he'd lost. His dreams had crumbled like the buildings of southern California. He would not be getting any money from the Chinese. His plan for a life of leisure was done before it was born. Now he was stuck with a broken country, a failed Presidency, and the death of the dysfunctional relationship with his wife. How to make some lemonade out of all of these lemons would be a huge trick – huge!

First things first; If he were to salvage his Presidency he must deal with the California situation. The place was gone; whoever was left would be dependent of the federal government. How many millions, no, billions would it cost? Where could he send them? How could they be supported? Who would pay the medical bills? The whole economy was already stretched to its limit. California's revenues were huge. If it were an independent nation, it would be the 9th largest in the world economically and now it was gone – gone. He would declare a national emergency – nationalize all industry and banking, recall all American forces around the world, secure the Southern border, then find someone to blame this all on – quickly.

Marty came in again - "Sir, some more bad news."

"Yes, Marty. For once I would like you to come in with some good news!"

"I wish I could Mister President. With the continuing catastrophic situation on the west coast, several states have indicated their intention to withdraw from the Union inasmuch as they know the country cannot withstand the anticipated financial and economic collapse. Texas, Arizona, New Mexico and Nevada have expressed their intentions on the floor of the House and Senate. There is rumor of some of the Southern states, Georgia, South Carolina, and could you believe it, Mississippi were also contemplating the same issue. Sir, if that happens, we're done. The domino effect will also include Utah, and Colorado then probably Virginia and Florida. If that happens throw in Louisiana and Arkansas – 13 states gone, Sir! If this happens the..."

"Marty", the President interrupted, "get everyone together now! Freeze every asset of every nation in our banks. The world owes us and I'm going to collect. We need to re-establish ourselves as the world leader we are. Freezing the assets and calling in our markers should provide us with sufficient capital to weather the storm and keep all of the renegade states in line."

The President paused and thought "What if a Senator and Congressman no longer had a state? Would they still be allowed to remain in office? This was getting very complicated – very.

Chapter Fifty-Two

LT Christmas was surprised. The Chinese pulled Frank from his room without benefit of guards and a single Chinese naval officer escorted him to the main building on the base in which they were housed. This was his first movement without a guard since he landed his plane on Hainan Island nearly one week ago.

He entered the office of the Commanding Officer, a Captain Fong, where he was asked to sit to wait for the Chinese naval officer. His escort departed the office, leaving Frank alone. Frank looked over the office and was surprised that, unlike most offices in the United States, this particular room did not contain the awards and pictures normally associated with an office of Captain Fong's rank. It was conspicuously bare of awards and pictures with only a large picture of Mao centered on the far wall.

Frank heard the door knob turn and Captain Fong entered the room. Frank remained in his chair.

"Is it not normal for an American naval officer of junior rank to stand when a senior officer enters the room?" the Chinese officer asked.

Frank immediately realized his lack of respect and stood. "Sorry sir, my apologies; LT Christmas, United States Navy at your service."

"Please be seated", Captain Fong stated. "LT Christmas I have both good news and bad news for you. The Chinese government is releasing you, your crew, and your aircraft back to American authorities as soon as the aircraft is fit to fly."

Frank could not believe it. He and the crew had only been in captivity for a week and then came this shot out of the blue. He made every attempt to conceal his pleasure but his elation could not be contained.

The Captain continued. "As I indicated, I also have bad news. Your country has experienced a catastrophic tragedy. A serious earthquake and follow on tsunami has devastated your west coast and resulted in the loss of millions of lives and complete destruction of your state of California. We, both I and the Chinese people, are compassionate and realize, when compared to the tragedy, that the mission of your aircraft and its violation of Chinese airspace is trivial. We assume that some of your crew may have lost family and their presence at their homes is of the utmost importance. Your crew has not been apprised of this information."

This second revelation nearly floored Frank; he could not believe the magnitude of the Captain's statement. "With all due respect Captain, are you telling me that the entire state of California has been devastated?" Frank asked.

"That is correct lieutenant. Your country has released only a few pictures and news reports, although sparse, indicate a high loss of life and the descriptions of the disaster are overwhelming. I will provide you all the information we have so that you may relay the data to your crew. We have announced to your President that you and your crew are being released and pledged our assistance to help the United States with humanitarian aid. Other countries from all parts of the world have applauded our kindness. Despite your propaganda against us, we are not the heartless people you depict. You may now return to your crew and provide the information which I have given you."

Frank rose from his chair in disbelief. He snapped to attention and said, "Captain Fong, on behalf of my crew, we appreciate your kindness for the treatment you have provided us and for your country's extension of aid to the United States."

"Very well, lieutenant. You are dismissed."

Frank's mind raced. First on his agenda would be breaking the news to his crew both in terms of their release and the catastrophe in California. Frank also thought of the SQUALL system and its intended compromise to the United States. Frank wondered if this mission was successful.

What Captain Fong had not informed Leiutenant Christmas was that he had been fully briefed on SQUALL and his country's ability to duplicate the system and its computer programs. The Chinese had what they believed was a fully functional SQUALL system, which, when they were finished, would allow them to keep U.S. submarines well off of China's coast. It would also ensure when they took control of the rebel Taiwanese that the U.S. would not be able to interfere. All that remained was a centralized command and control location from which to deploy and operate – and that would be Hainan.

When China was satisfied with the operation of SQUALL, it would turn the system over to its Communist allies, Russia and North Korea for further reproduction and usage. Soon they would control the seas and be able to fully thwart the U.S. submaring and missile system operations.

Chapter Fifty-Three

Paul Webster fumed. He'd seen all sorts of unscrupulous activities in D.C.; it was the way of life for him, his contemporaries, his friends and even his enemies. Scandals, treacherous double and triple crosses had to be considered the norm, but never an assorted mess as this.

The President of the United States had committed treason, committed it with reckless abandon and he was, in all probability, going to get away with it – another sell out to the almighty dollar. From the environmentalist, with emphasis on "mental", to the Far Left and Right, there was corruption on all sides. Even if the Story action was open for all to know, the public wouldn't do anything about it. Webster had never been so totally neutralized in all his life. Maybe he'd change his mind about being President. He'd concluded the only way to fix it was for the whole thing to come crashing down. Not likely. More probably, we'd just erode away into national insignificance – rot and fall from the tree of nations into oblivion. The great experiment over. Not because of a flaw in the design, but because of the flaw in the men who abrogated their sworn duty.

How could he have forgotten? As a child, his mother told him the story from the Bible of the Garden of Eden.

It didn't fail because of a design flaw but for a human flaw. Nothing had changed over all thousands of years, mankind's mindset was, and probably always would be, to promote self above all else.

If the Chinese had SQUALL, what else had they gotten? Would they, with the missile technology, commit the dreaded first strike? With SQUALL, they could render our ballistic missile silos impotent, and if the Sino-Soviet link was rebuilt, the U.S. would be obliterated either through threat or in reality. He should tell the President himself – his mind was racing. He was nearly in a panic state. He'd chased this very scenario all his adult life and now that he had it – what? The only thing he'd be President of is a North America dung heap – NO THANKS!

Options, Paul. What were the options? Think man think!" But he couldn't. Oh, God. He fell to his knees. What next? Help me. No! Forgive me and my countrymen for the folly we've brought to our door. America no more; it was more than he could stand. He wept for all of those things in life he'd passed on pursuing his empire. Oh, forgive me, please!

Chapter Fifty-Four

Frank was returned to his quarters and immediately was reunited with LTJG Salerno and CWO4 Cutler. He informed them of the entire situation. Yes, they were being released but they would be returning to a country that was less than whole.

The elation of returning home was obviously tempered by the situation. Between the three of them, it was understood that at least 3 of the crew called southern California home, a home that was no longer there.

None of them knew the extent of damage or the current condition of the aircraft but the Chinese Communist Captain had indicated to Frank that they would fly the aircraft back to Okinawa. Frank and his co-pilot knew the P3 was damaged and American parts would be needed to repair the plane; what was not clear was where the parts were coming from and how long it would take for their delivery. Frank had already decided to remain with his aircraft and Mark immediately volunteered to stay; it would only take the two of them to fly the aircraft. CWO4 Cutler would accompany the remainder of the crew back to Okinawa via whatever means that was provided. The plan would obviously have to be approved by both the Chinese and the American chain of command.

The immediate concern however, was to inform the crew of the information the three officers had and exactly how to share it. Accordingly, Frank opened the door of the quarters and asked the Chinese guard if they could now talk with the remainder of the crew.

Within minutes the three American naval officers were led to a mess hall type area where the crew had been gathered. When they entered the room, the crew cheered in anticipation of good news. This was the first time the officers and crew had been in contact since they were led away from the P-3.

Frank addressed the crew. "Shipmates, we are going home!" he started.

Bedlam broke out. Cheers, hugs, tears, and laughter permeated the entire room. A few of his crew bowed their heads in prayer, thanking God for keeping them safe throughout the entire ordeal. After all, they had survived an air collision with another plane, a frightful flight over an angry sea, a forced landing in a Communist country, and a harrowing week of capture by a heretofore fearful enemy. Now they were going to return home. Divine guidance must have intervened.

Frank let them carry on for about five minutes before passing on the rest of the news. "OK, quiet down, quiet down. I have further information to pass on."

The crew returned to their seats.

Frank began again. "Along with the great news, I have to pass on additional information which, before the thought enters your mind, has nothing to do with our release. Our country has experienced a severe tragedy which has caused the death of an uncountable number of our citizens and destruction of whole cities. Two earthquakes and a series of tidal waves have completely devastated California."

The three crewmembers from Southern California immediately reacted.

"Lieutenant, what do you mean devastated southern California?"

Frank tried to explain himself. He told them that Las Angeles, San Diego, and San Francisco were virtually gone as was most of the area south of the San Andreas fault. Little was left standing in any of the cities and casualty numbers were off the chart. He promised those who had relatives and friends in those areas would receive priority for return to the states. He would also ensure that, as information became available, he would keep them informed. Fortunately, those crewmembers who resided in southern California did not originate from those immediate areas.

Frank continued. That is all the information I currently have. The Chinese have been most courteous and I expect to have more information as the day goes on. I will be making every attempt to contact members of our chain of command and act as the liaison between our government and the Chinese. I promise all of you that I will pass on any and all information that I receive as soon as I can get it back to you. I stand proud of you all and I will ensure our entire chain of command is aware of the outstanding job all of you performed before, after, and during our mission."

Frank wished he had more to tell them. He was happy that the three members of the crew from California were not directly affected by the earthquake; he would have

afforded themj priority in getting them home if they had have been. It was the least he could have done.

So far, "Mission Accomplished". I got the plane here, the crew here safely and they are returning safely, the Chicoms got SQUALL and we are all going home. Wonder what that will be like, he thought.

Chapter Fifty-Five

Sam closed his eyes – it was done and Frank was alive. The Chinese had contacted the President directly with an offer of humanitarian aid and the release of Frank and his crew. Unlike the Chinese, they had conveyed the triviality of the captured crew when compared to the seriousness of the natural disaster. It was so unlike the Chinese. President Story had called Frank directly from Air Force One just finished discussing the situation. The date of Frank's return had not been agreed upon but it would be soon.

Sam thanked God and then called Kitty.

"Frank is OK. President Story called and said the Chinese would be releasing him and his crew within days. He is still being held on Hainan Island but the State Department is on it and they figure their release will occur within a few days.

Kitty wept with joy. For the past week, she had recounted Frank's entire life from the very first day at the orphanage through his graduation at the Naval Academy, flight school and up to his capture by the Chinese. She was not sure whether she would ever see him again. Now it would be a joyful homecoming.

"That has to be the greatest news I have heard in a long time. I will call Jen and let her know right away," Kitty gushed. "Sam, I love you."

"Right back at you."

- Kitty hung up and then immediately dialed Jen. When Jen answered, Kitty relayed the entire story to Jen and, as Kitty had thought, they both cried in relief. Through their tears they even began planning Frank's homecoming.

The television was turned on and in the background another "Breaking News" news flash was being described. After so many of these occurring in the past twelve hours, many people had become complacent and all she heard was something about President Story.

Kitty thought out loud. "The President what?". The President had done something but she missed the report almost completely.

Then the telephone rang again. She picked up the telephone and said, "Hello, Colby residence".

Chapter Fifty-Six

The knock at the door could barely be heard over the jet noise of the aircraft.

"Come in", President Story responded.

A full bird Colonel entered the room with his head down indicating the bearing of bad news. He took a deep breath.

"Let it go, Colonel, it can't be anything worse that what I have heard so far today", the President said.

"Sir, we have made contact with a member of your wife's security detail and we have confirmed that she has died during the collapse of her hotel during the night; her body was discovered a little while ago. She died instantaneously. My sincerest condolences sir."

"Thank you Colonel for both the report and your condolences."

As the Colonel departed the room, the President thought that that put a period to another chapter in his life. He thought out loud, "Good-bye Jane, at one time in my life, I loved you dearly and I thank you for those good times."

Chapter Fifty-Seven

While enroute to Nevada, the President continued to make decisions concerning the country but his mind was elsewhere. The trip was mind boggling; the condition of the country left a lot to be desired. The P-3 incident with the Chinese was solved; out-of-the-blue, the Chinese decided to return the crew and aircraft because of the situation in California. Good for them; helped his situation with little or no intervention and they obviously were unaware of the SQUALL situation. If the President had carried his term through, this would be a major intelligence coup that would remain however, classified to the highest levels; so much for that.

President Story could not do much about the California situation; it was an act of God that he could not have anticipated. Vice President Cord would have to earn his pay for this one. After all, he sat around for years and did nothing! The next few months would truly make up for that!

Once on the ground in Nevada, Steven Story reverted to his civilian side and worked his private telephone lines. The only thing which interested him now was the status of a rather large deposit to his private account in the Cayman

Islands. He had made his decision and as soon as the he confirmed the status of his deposit, he was out. No cover, no story.

His private telephone rang; he picked up. "Done.", he was told.

President Story used all the confusion created by the earthquakes, his wife's death and the landing of Air force One in Nevada to liberate himself from his security team and find the time to get out of Dodge. He boarded a private jet and began his journey, winging his way to Espirito Santo, Brazil. He had been working on the purchase of a large estate in Brazil for months; clandestinely, completely without the use of his name. He would have all he wanted; privacy, easy access to flights anywhere in the world and no one would know until he landed. **He had initially planned to divorce his wife and give her enough cash to temper her golas and keep her mouth shut for ever. The earthquake however, took care of that and left more money in his account.** The only thing remained was to rid himself of the burden of his office.

In a taped speech now being released, soon to be ex-President Story presented his adieu in a single paragraph to the American people.

"My fellow Americans, today we have suffered a colossal failure that has – and will continue to cripple the country's ability to defend its interests around the world. It happened on my watch as I was distracted by issues occurring in my personal life. Therefore, in the best interests of the country, and in order to ensure preservation of the nation, I have tendered my resignation as President of the United States, effective

midnight tonight. I wish you all well. God bless you and God bless America."

He knew the country would be shocked but he would be airborne and unavailable for contact. He had filed false flight plans and there would be so much turmoil that by the time the country figured things out, it would be too late. He'd beaten them all, the Republicans, the Democrats, the liberals, the independents. Most precious to him, he'd beaten the press! He would never forget this day; it was a "Story book" finish. He laughed out loud and picked up the phone.

There was another little twist to his plan. His pilot had filed a flight plan for Espiritu Santo but instead of flying southeast, his jet was heading almost due west to the New Hebrides – 600 miles west of Fiji; 1200 miles from Australia. When he landed, he would no longer be Steven Story but rather a rich recluse who had no desire to associate with others. This island was remote and dual-ruled by Britain and France and his comings and goings could be easily concealed. He hadn't felt this good since he was the Governor. They would he his laughter echoing throughout the halls of the White House for years to come.

The pilot of the aircraft came on the intercom. "Please fasten your seat belts. We are going to experience some rather heavy turbulence for the next few minutes."

Chapter Fifty-Eight

Sam got the news just before it broke in on all of the TV stations. President Story had resigned! What more could happen to this country! We go from an international incident with the Chinese to a natural disaster effecting millions of our people to the resignation of a coward President who deserted his own country in a time of its greatest need. The country was in turmoil.

Just then Paul Webster barged into his office."

"Colby, I don't agree with you on next to nothing but, I don't doubt your loyalty to the nation, nor your dedication to preserve it. That asshole Story, may he rot in hell…." The telephone rang. Sam put the incoming call on speaker.

"Sam, John. More information; I know you heard about POTUS but that isn't the worst of this evolution. His private plane went down about two hundred miles off the coast of California and there were no survivors. According to the flight plan, he was on his way to Brazil. Why he was off the California coast is anybody's guess. We'll never know the full extent of the damage he's done. Alec Cord has just been sworn in as President."

Webster muttered that the loss of Story was probably a plus.

John Cunningham continued, "The leadership of both houses is on their way in with the Justices. We've got one grand mess here and the cancer must have been deep – 6 Senators and 18 Congressmen have resigned and every one of them is trying to get out of the country. Cord is clueless and the press is bearing down. What now?"

Sam motioned for Webster to sit down.

"What now? We have to pull this country together to stop the hemorrhaging and keep the country from collapse. We have plenty of braniacs to make it happen. We have to keep the citizens of this great land calm and let them know that the government is in charge. That is what we have to do."

Chapter Fifty-Nine

Hua smiled. To quote the great American author, "the report of my death was a great exaggeration". While scheduled to be in California, he had missed his flight and remained in his homeland. Everyone made the assumption that he was in Los Angeles when the earthquake and when not being able to account for him, the Americans had assumed his death.

The American President had a price – as did everyone. Finding it was the key and there were none better than Li Jaing Hua. He was sure once the President was out of the U.S. the Chinese could compromise him so easily that they would recover more than half of the money they had given him. His weakness for young girls was well known as was his reliance on cocaine. Yes, his lot was sealed.

Hua felt sure his promotion would give him much latitude in the selection of his successor, and he liked Captain Fong. Fong was a dog but a loyal one. He knew where and how things got done and he'd make a perfect Ambassador; military bodyguard – ruthless and determined. His weakness was his inability to control and project power.

The western way of life would keep Fong busy for years and provide a loyal backer. While the Chinese philosophy did not have room for decadence, Fong would become mesmerized by the availability of just about everything in the United States. Hua knew; after all, he had experienced it for years. He allowed himself a self-congratulatory smile. His years of paying attention to every detail were finally paying off. Not bad, a U.S. President in his pocket!

Hua would one day be in line for the Party Chair if things kept going this way. He made a mental note to ensure President Story had a few young pretty house keepers to keep him occupied for a few months. Once he was situated, Hua would announce about the decadent President and the return of 50 million dollars would surely catapult him to the head table with the Chairman and allow him to influence China for decades to come. Happy, happy, happy, happy talk – he'd found Bali Hai, and all by himself. "Hua, you devil."

"Lee Fung," he snapped. "My bath!"

Lee Fung entered the room. "Ambassador Hua, I have news. The disgraced President of the United States was killed in a plane crash a few hours ago."

Hua's dreams were shattered. Now only he knew of the President's turn coat ways. His mind drifted to the $50 million dollars that had been transferred to the former President's account in the Cayman Islands. "How do I explain such a loss", he muttered.

Chapter Sixty

Without thought, the Chinese **technicians** had **immediately and,** successfully copied the SQUALL software and incorporated it into their Command and Control systems. What a magnificent program; its ability to track and control submarine missile systems was almost beyond their comprehension. Soon, they would be able to track and eliminate the major forces of the U.S. Pacific Submarine Fleet. **With their shipbuilding program centered on the production of nuclear missile submarines and with the SQUALL software, China would soon be without a viable adversary in anti-submarine warfare and they would control the seas in years to come. In the near future, the software would be provided to the Soviet Union and North Korea. The U.S. Navy's supremacy on the seas would soon be over!**

Coincident to the Chinese government incorporating the SQUALL system into their communications hierarchy, the computer virus was **unknowingly** set. No anti-virus program known to man could stop it. Every test, every opening of the system would prove functional. Only when migrated to a new system would the virus become active. Then slowly – ever so slowly – it would first work its way through every system that it was connected to, over 7-8 months it should have penetrated every Chinese Naval ASW system of the centrally run Chinese military. Once there, it would be dormant for 30 days, then imperceptibly, at first, it would start its degradation by miscalculating the vital locating data sending ships and air craft hundreds of miles off the contact. Frustrated pilots and ship's captains would spend countless days retracing missed contacts only to find they could not relocate anything. Operators of the system would be accused of stupidity and ineptness – command centers would have wholesale removals – all the experience of the Chinese ASW defense system degraded to total paralysis in action. U.S. subs could then resume the dominant position and exercise their ability to rain down fire with impunity. Yes, the risk had been well worth it – but for how long?

U. S. politics and politicians have all sold out. The Chinese weren't the only ones in need of a house cleaning. The American people had better wake up or face their total collapse. A collapse so total and devastating it would never recover; and the real scary part, not a shot need be fired. The press had played a major role in electing leaders and Presidents for years. Along with the abject failure of the American public to stay informed and their united effort to sell soft socialism/communism as American values.

Those pompous self-aggrandizing fools; you can't keep an anaconda as a pet and sleep with it. You won't like it when it decides you're its next meal, but by then it's too late. The press had hand fed this snake one time too many. It almost got them. Sadly they'd never know.

Chapter Sixty-One

Frank rolled over. The dream kept coming back. How long would be and Jenny have? Would they ever have a chance?

Frank **would resign** his commission when he returned home from Hainan Island. **Currently, his most important concern was his crew, their well-being and their subsequent return to the Unites States. While by no means a diplomat, his determined discussions with the Chinese nationals resulted in the waiving of much of the red tape and the crew had been sent home within days of their release.** The U.S. government brought a 707 jet to Hainan Island and returned the crew to Okinawa where they were treated like returning heroes. **Each individual would be facing lengthy debriefing by U.S. officials from various organizations of the government. At least, the crew would be provided ample time to be re-acquainted with their families and loved ones.**

CWO4 Cutler returned to the United States immediately after returning to Okinawa; he didn't spend one day on the island before being transported back to Maryland. He had **an immediate** date for debriefings with the National Security Agency.

Frank and Mark Salerno remained on Hainan for nearly two weeks. They both went over their plane the utmost care and detailed the list of required parts needed to repair the aircraft for flight. **A crew of** American aircraft maintenance technicians flew in on the relief aircraft to aid in the **salvage and repair.** Two additional flights with spare parts **were** needed to get the aircraft ready to go home. The largest replace part was, of course, the propeller which was destroyed when the Chinese J-8 collided with the P-3.

The American maintenance crew worked nearly around the clock as none of them wanted to spend any more time than necessary on Hainan Island. The plane was finally cleared to fly and, not wasting any time, Frank and Mark came aboard for the return flight. It was pretty obvious to them that the Chinese had conducted a thorough inspection and review of all parts of the P-3 specifically the monitoring and intercept equipment in the rear of the aircraft. When the wheels finally went up and the aircraft was feet wet, little mattered. They were headed home.

The aircraft performed flawlessly and within hours they were approaching Okinawa. Once the P-3 touched down and taxied briefly to the hanger, both pilots breathed a sigh of relief. They were home.

The aircraft was greeted by a bevy of Navy brass as well as a horde of Navy technicians. The aircraft would be completed isolated and thoroughly reviewed electronically to ensure no Chinese "bugs" were attached to the aircraft and equipment. It was very unlikely that any of the computer equipment would ever be used again to ensure to viruses were planted in the equipment.

The Navy brass greeted LT Christmas with a crisp salute and a firm handshake. Their next statement was almost out of an I Love Lucy show, "you have a lot of splaining to do!" And he did. Most of the "brass" meeting him knew nothing of his mission; he would be debriefed in Sensitive Compartmented Information Facility (SCIF) by those with a need-to-know. He knew today was the day that he would conduct their final debrief.

He couldn't wait to see Jenny **but he knew that would have to wait; duty first.** He thanked God for her and vowed to never leave her side. Wherever and whatever happened, he was not leaving her again.

Chapter Sixty-Two

He was a fish out of water; an American in a land where round-eyes were one in a million. It was difficult to remain anonymous with white skin in a land of yellow; some of the most beautiful women in the world; some the poorest people on the planet. It was, indeed, a much stranger place than the East Coast of the United States where he could melt into a crowd without difficulty

He was a business man who carried a briefcase; a briefcase altered to conceal the true intent of his business. His briefcase carried a specially designed .223 caliber rifle; equipped with a sniper's scope and special ammunition. His target, a former Chinese ambassador to the United States; one who had partnered with a corrupt government employee; one who had been in the middle of the downfall of the President of the United States. He succeeded with his quest and was the only remaining human who was intimately aware of the occurrences surrounding President Steven Story.

The crosshairs of the sniper's scope was centered on its target approximately 500 yards distant. It would not be an easy shot as the target was surrounded by the harlots of his present life. The target was one of the few who benefitted from and traitorous deceit of both his own government and that of the United States. His erasure would provide closure to a dark era for the United States.

The businessman's finger slowly closed over the trigger and produced the minimal stress to fire the weapon.

Former Ambassador Hua was no more.

Chapter Sixty-Three

The political situation in the United States was a shambles. Senator Paul Webster had assumed a leadership role in trying to bring the system back to its original purpose.

Immediately after the resignation and death of President Story and the swearing in of Alex Cord, Senator Webster stormed in to the Oval Office and demanded that President Cord submit his resignation and get out of D.C. within an hour or face the most grueling public Grand Jury hearing in the history of the Republic. Whether it was ignorance, incompetence, or both, Cord was not fit to be the President of these United States.

The same would go for the House leadership and Speaker Pro tempore of the Senate – all of them bungling idiots. He used the Supreme Court to establish martial law across the United States until which time that some resemblance of law and order could be established. Once that was done, he'd deal with the states; the people would need a strong non-partisan leader and he was the only one there was. The central government, though near collapse, must sustain a strong front; all three branches of the government would have to work together; damn the partisan politics. Times were going to rough for quite a while; people might balk at first but strong leadership would ensure the direction of the country. Time to think America over again, but how to instill patriotism? The schools had all bought into the "bad America", been fed the liberal poison – What a mess! Who could he trust? Colby, for sure. Who else? Where were the patriots?

He remembered... "When in the course of human events it becomes necessary..."

"Blair, get me Sam Colby on the phone. I also need Chief Justice Baker and the Joint Chiefs. Then we'll need all of the state Governors. We're going to have to rebuild the whole thing. I also want that P-3 pilot Frank Christmas, like it or not he's the new force in America and we'd better be sure we get him off on the right foot. Notify the press that until further notice all articles relating in any way to the government, its state or future, will be first run through our office. Blair, hand pick a staff to filter it all – we're badly wounded, Blair but not mortally, yet. If we can hold off for 48-72 hours, we can steady up and hold course until we're self-sufficient again. The military will ensure commerce runs and the Fed will monitor the finances. It's just the politicians we're going to have to watch out for. What's left of them, all think they should be President."

Chapter Sixty-Four

It was May 25th. Sand Military Academy just completed its graduation and a certain fraternity brother was already being summoned to Washington, D. C.

God bless America.

What was this all about?

Printed in the United States
By Bookmasters